More Super SCARY STORIES for Sleep-Overs

By Q. L. Pearce

Illustrated by Dwight Been

Lowell House
House
Juvenile
Los Angeles

To Beth and Beny.
—Q.L.P.

To my brothers and sisters.
—D.M.B.

ISBN: 1-56565-563-X

Library of Congress Catalog Card Number is available.

Designed by Michele Lanci-Altomare

Manufactured in the United States of America

10 9 8 7 6 5 4 3 2

Contents

Legend

Mystical flute music drifted out through the open doors of the new shop on River Street.

"This place must have just opened," Robyn's cousin Sabrina commented, peering into the large display window. "It looks like it has some neat stuff. Want to check it out?"

"Sure," Robyn said with a shrug.

"OK," her friend Julie chimed in. "But let's make it really quick. I want to eat lunch. I'm starving."

"You're always starving," Robyn commented with a smile as the three girls entered the shop.

Willowbrook was a small town. Still, it was right between the Klamath River and Redwood National Park, so there were always plenty of tourists, campers, and fishermen around to keep businesses booming in the midtown shopping area known as the Village.

"Wow," Sabrina said softly once inside the shop. "This is cool." A wide range of Native American crafts, dolls, clothing, and other items were on display. Some stood on rough wooden shelves, while others were heaped in colorful baskets atop a glass showcase in the center of the room. Robyn studied the delicate silver necklaces strung with pink and white shells that were carefully arranged in the case. She loved jewelry.

Julie inspected the baskets. "These are so pretty," she observed as she ran her finger around the curved edge of a basket that held a variety of pine- and floral-scented incense.

"And so finely woven that you can even carry water in them without spilling a drop," came a voice from the rear of the shop. A nice-looking, dark-haired young man stepped toward them. "May I help you, ladies?"

"No, thank you," Robyn answered politely. "We're in the village every week, but we hadn't seen this store before. We're just taking a quick look."

"Ah," he said with a grin. "You must be local residents. I am all the more pleased to meet you. My name is Henry, and my grandmother and I own this shop." He made a sweeping gesture toward the displays. "As you can see, we specialize in the traditional products and crafts of the tribes of this area . . . my people, the Shasta, among them."

"It's really nice," Robyn said sincerely. "We'll be back again when we have more time."

"Just one more moment," he said as he plucked a small

plastic bag from one of the display baskets. "These are sugar pine nuts. They're very tasty." He held them out to Julie. "Please accept them as a small introductory gift. And tell your friends about us," he added.

"He was nice," Julie said, rummaging for another handful of pine nuts as they walked toward the pizza parlor.

Suddenly Robyn stopped. "Wait!" She patted both of her jacket pockets. "I don't have my wallet. I must have set it down on the counter when I was looking at the necklaces. You guys go ahead and get in line for a table. I'll run back and get it."

But when she got back to the store, Robyn was disappointed to see that her wallet wasn't on the counter. She searched around the floor, but it wasn't there either.

"Is this what you are looking for?"

Startled, Robyn looked up to see a petite woman standing behind the glass counter, holding her wallet. The woman's long gray hair was pulled back in a tight braid, and her brown face was wrinkled with age.

"Yes," Robyn answered. "That's my wallet."

"My grandson found it," the old woman explained. "He thought you might be back for it shortly."

"Thank you," Robyn responded.

As she reached for the wallet, Robyn's gaze fell on a pendant in the case that she had not noticed earlier. It was a polished, jet-black stone on a chain of delicate silver links that were so fine they looked almost fluid. An intricate design was carved deeply into the crescent-shaped stone. "That necklace is really beautiful," she remarked, pointing to the jewelry. "What kind of stone is that?"

"Obsidian," the woman answered, slipping the piece

7

from the case and holding it up to the light. "It is a kind of volcanic glass. It was once highly prized by the Karok people who lived here. Would you like to try it on?"

"Well," Robyn said hesitantly. "My friends *are* waiting for me." *They're probably going to have to stand in line for a while,* she thought. "Sure," she finally answered. "I'd love to try it on."

Looking in the mirror, Robyn admired the way the polished stone reflected the light. "I've never seen anything like this necklace," she said appreciatively. "Is it one-of-a-kind?"

"There is one other," the woman whispered with an air of mystery. "It holds a stone that can sustain life indefinitely for the wearer. The necklace you have on contains merely a powerless duplicate."

Robyn was intrigued. She didn't protest as the old woman began to relate the legend of the stone.

"Our people, the Shasta, have traded with the Karok since the time when the great trees rose everywhere like prayers to the spirits of nature. This is a story from those early times."

Robyn fingered the pendant as the shopkeeper spoke.

"Three centuries ago, a young Karok girl became enraged with a boy of the tribe who did not return her affection for him," she began. "When he was promised to another, the girl could not control her fury. She lured the boy to his death on a hillside trail, where he was buried by a rock slide of her making. But the girl's dreadful deed was witnessed by a member of her tribe who had been hunting nearby."

"That's horrible," Robyn said with a gasp. "What happened to her?"

"That very night, the tribe was called to gather around a

8

council fire. The girl was brought to face the tribal shaman, a powerful medicine man. As she stood trembling in the flickering firelight, the shaman decreed that her punishment was to be banished to the forest to live in solitude, with nothing to do but think about her terrible crime."

"So, what about the pendant?" Robyn asked. "How does it fit into the story?"

The woman leaned slightly forward on the glass counter. "The shaman's magic was very strong. He wanted the girl to truly suffer. To ensure this, he placed a carved obsidian pendant around her neck, one that could never be removed by her own hand. Dark in color as her own black heart, the pendant kept the spirit of death away, making the punishment everlasting. The shaman then commanded the girl to return to the scene of her crime once each century at midnight on the first night of the harvest moon. In this way she was doomed to remember what she had done."

"Where was this place—the scene of the crime, I mean?" Robyn asked with growing curiosity. "Is it around here?"

The shopkeeper nodded slowly. "It is. But even the animals of the forest will not go near it."

Robyn raised an eyebrow. "Well, living forever doesn't sound like such an awful punishment."

"Some things are not worth the price that one must pay," the woman responded solemnly.

For a moment Robyn felt as if the woman knew something else, some important detail about the punishment that she wasn't telling. With a shrug, she removed the pendant. She had lost her fascination with it once she learned that it was only an imitation. Instead, she bought a small book on local Native American legends, one that included the tale the shopkeeper had told her.

At home that night she read the story again. The editor of the book had included a footnote explaining how he had tried to determine the exact location and time frame of the Karok girl's next legendary return. "No way!" Robyn exclaimed after reading the footnote for the second time. Then she excitedly checked her calendar.

"I can't believe this!" she gasped. "If the editor is right, the girl is supposed to return only three weeks from now!" Turning off the light, she made her way over to her bedroom window and gazed out at the moon. "I wonder if it could be true." she whispered. "I wonder what it would be like to know you were going to live forever." As she spoke, a cloud overtook the moon, blocking out its pale light and plunging the nearby forest into sinister darkness.

• • • • • • • • • • •

By the time the harvest moon rose over the horizon three weeks later, Robyn had come up with a plan to satisfy her gnawing curiosity about whether the story the shopkeeper had told her was true. She even toyed with the fantasy of somehow winning the pendant for herself. Following the clues in the book, she had already discovered the site of an ancient rock slide in the forest that seemed to match the description of the place where the boy had died. She hadn't told anyone about her scheme to be at the spot exactly at the stroke of midnight on the appointed day. No one would believe the story anyway, she told herself. *It's only a legend,* they would say. Robyn had said it herself many times, but somewhere deep inside she felt as if maybe, just maybe it could be true . . . and she was going to find out.

Later that night Robyn waited until she was certain that her parents were asleep. Then she slipped out through her window, got on her bicycle, which she'd hidden in the bushes, and took off toward the forest, her heavy breathing forming tiny white clouds in the chill autumn air.

Turning off the main road, Robyn followed a rutted dirt trail for a few hundred yards, then stopped to prop her bicycle against a small tree.

Taking a flashlight from her backpack, she checked her watch. It was eleven o'clock.

Cautiously she made her way through the forest. She'd grown up around here and had been alone in the forest many times, but never at night. The light of the full moon made the large boulders that rested here and there stand out like pale, grotesque phantoms. All around, the inky shadows slowly shifted as the lunar orb made its way across the night sky.

Finally she reached a small clearing against the low hillside she had been heading for. As the shopkeeper had predicted, it was completely deserted, as if even the animals refused to go near it. At the center of the clearing was a jumble of rocks and boulders that had probably tumbled down the hillside long ago. Robyn wondered for a moment if the bones of an unfortunate young Karok Indian boy still rested under them. She settled into a wide, shadowy space between two boulders and switched off her flashlight.

Everything was so still and quiet. The long walk had made her tired, and though Robyn tried to resist, she felt her eyelids droop as she slowly drifted into a light sleep.

A low moan woke her, and she snatched up her flashlight. Then she froze as she heard the noise again.

Trembling from the cold night air and her growing fright, Robyn hunched farther down in her hiding place. *What am I doing here?* she thought desperately. *This was a crazy idea.* Now the moan was replaced by a soft wailing sound . . . and it was coming closer.

Finally her curiosity overcame her fear. Robyn silently leaned forward and peeked out. Her eyes widened in horror. There, only a few yards away at the edge of the clearing, stood a young girl in the same type of Karok garb that had been illustrated in the book Robyn had read. The girl was sobbing pitifully, and clawing at something around her neck. With a shock of recognition, Robyn gazed at the carved obsidian pendant glimmering hypnotically in the moonlight. It appeared to resist every attempt that the tortured girl made to remove it. Finally the cursed maiden fell to the ground and howled in anguish.

It's true! Robyn realized. *It's all true.* Thinking only of the pendant and its incredible power, she eased out of her hiding place and moved slowly, inch by inch, toward the writhing girl. Robyn's eyes were glued to the gleaming black stone. She had to have it.

With a sudden start the girl looked up, but Robyn didn't pause to see the agony in her dark eyes. She just reached greedily for the pendant and yanked it brutally away. All at once the pain seemed to melt from the Karok girl, and for a

fleeting moment she smiled. With a final glance at the moon she closed her eyes and dissolved into a pile of dust. Robyn watched as the fine grains stirred, then were carried off in the gentle night breeze.

In triumph, Robyn gripped the obsidian stone in her fist. "Now *I* will live forever!" she cried out. She opened her hand slowly. Trembling, she draped the broken chain around her own neck and instantly felt the stone at her throat grow warm . . . then hot. It was as if the pendant were burning itself into her skin.

"What's happening?" she cried, trying to reach for it, but Robyn's arms were becoming rigid, and against her will they were now reaching toward the night sky. Terrified, she felt her body stiffen and stretch, as her feet sank into the ground and her skin thickened and grew hard.

All at once, Robyn realized the truth. She suddenly knew the vital detail that the shopkeeper had neglected to tell her. It was that the Karok girl regained her human form only once each century. The rest of the time she lived in a different form—the one that Robyn's body was now taking. "No!" she screamed in the last vestiges of her human voice. "I didn't know it would be like this! Please!" she begged. But her voice faded away into nothing more than a soft lament that sounded almost like the wind moaning through the treetops. And as the animals of the night watched from the distant shadows, they saw a new tree take root and become a part of the ancient forest. But unlike the other trees, this one would live forever.

The Colony

ndrea's mother opened the curtains. "Time to get up, sleepyhead!" she announced cheerfully.

Blinking her eyes, Andrea flung her hands over her head and happily stretched her long, lean body. The sunlight streaming through the now open sliding glass doors of the motel balcony had the opposite effect on her older sister, Claire. Claire pulled the covers over her head.

"Morning, Mom," Andrea said, sliding out of bed and stepping out on the balcony. "Morning, grouch," she called to her sister, still hiding from the day.

The family had been vacationing in the Florida Keys for three days, and Andrea was still awed by the spectacular view. Their motel was nestled at the inner edge of a beautiful white-sand beach. Beyond were the placid, azure waters of the Gulf of Mexico.

"Your dad and I have already had breakfast and your brother is already down on the beach," her mom told her. Andrea dropped her gaze and immediately spotted Brandon wading along the shore, snorkeling gear in hand.

"He's not going in the water without me!" Andrea squealed, racing to get ready. "Come on, Claire," she urged, pulling on her still-damp swimsuit. "Are you going to sleep all day? Brandon's outside already having fun. Let's go!"

"I'll be down in a few minutes," Claire mumbled.

Moments later, Andrea sprinted across the warm sand and charged into the water up to her knees. Seeing her brother farther out with his mask and snorkel on, floating facedown on the surface, Andrea watched as he curled down in a shallow dive. Seconds later he popped up just a few feet away, blowing a stream of water from his snorkel. Then tugging off his mask, he began sloshing toward her.

"Look at this!" Brandon said proudly when he reached her. He held up a cone-shaped, brown-and-white shell that was as large as his hand.

"Wow, it's beautiful," Andrea declared.

"Hey, you guys! What have you got?" Claire asked, joining them in the water.

"It's a cool shell," Brandon answered. "It's the only neat one I've found so far," he added.

"You're just not looking in the right place," Claire said matter-of-factly.

"Oh really?" Brandon shot back. "And since when did you become the expert?"

"Since I talked to that guy up there." She gestured toward a tall man walking up the beach carrying two large red plastic buckets. "He had lots of really pretty shells. I asked him where they came from and he said he'd collected them along a cove about half a mile from here, closer to the Atlantic side. It's overgrown and it doesn't have a nice beach, so people rarely go there."

"That won't bother me," Andrea responded with a big smile. "Let's check it out."

Claire held up her hand. "Wait a minute. He said something else, too. There's a steep drop-off, and the current can shift sometimes. He warned me not to go there, but if I did, to stay close to shore—and he was serious about it. He said *not* to go beyond the drop-off for any reason."

"OK," Brandon said, nodding.

"No problem," Andrea agreed. "Let's go."

It didn't take long for the kids to find the cove the man had told Claire about, even though a stand of scrub pines hid it from the main road and a tangle of vegetation covered the beach almost all the way to the waterline. Only a thin strip of coarse yellowish sand remained uncovered.

I don't like this, she thought, slapping at a mosquito that was making a meal on her blood. "The guy who told you about this place was right, Claire," she said when they reached the beach. "It doesn't look that great."

"Not if you want to play volleyball," Brandon said with a chuckle. "But we're here to snorkel."

Andrea couldn't shake the edgy feeling that had

gripped her. Still, she waded into the clear blue water. It was much deeper than the beach where they usually swam, and it sloped more steeply.

Claire eased out beside her and Andrea noticed that her sister was still wearing the pearl ring that their parents had given her on her last birthday. "Did you mean to wear your good ring into the water?" Andrea asked.

"Oh, no," Claire muttered. "I forgot to take it off at the motel." She looked back at the beach. "I don't feel safe leaving it there. I'll just have to wear it.

Adjusting her snorkel in her mouth, Andrea stretched out facedown on the surface to view the underwater realm. The sand was dotted with patches of coral, each patch alive with colorful fish.

Andrea caught a flash of silver out of the corner of her eye. She turned just in time to see a small barracuda, its gaping mouth filled with tiny, sharp teeth. The predatory fish circled them curiously for a moment, then swam gracefully seaward. Andrea watched it until something in the deep water beyond the drop-off drew her attention.

What is that? she wondered, peering into the shadowy depths where little sunlight penetrated. It looked like a structure of some kind, almost like a sunken fortress. Whatever it was, it didn't appear to be a natural formation . . . and something about it seemed sinister.

Andrea wanted to get a better look. Kicking a little closer, she took a deep breath and dove down a few feet. She kicked again, propelling herself even deeper and closer to the edge. Then to her astonishment, she was just able to make out an ancient-looking door at the base of the

structure . . . and the door was opening! Andrea gasped and her mouth filled with seawater. Fighting the reflex to swallow, she rocketed upward, back into the bright sunlight.

Coughing and sputtering, she tugged off her mask.

"You OK?" Brandon called out to her.

"I swallowed some water. Let's go in," Andrea choked out, heading for shore.

"Did you see that thing in the deep water?" she asked the others as they all flopped down on the sand.

"You mean the weird stone thing?" Brandon responded. "Yeah, I don't know why, but it kind of gave me the creeps."

"Me, too," Andrea admitted. "I saw . . . I mean I thought I saw . . ." she hesitated. "Did you guys see a part of it open?"

"I think you've been holding your breath too long," Claire said, laughing.

Andrea scowled. "Lots of spooky things happen around here," she declared defensively. "I've read stories about people and ships disappearing without a trace in a part of the Atlantic Ocean called the Bermuda Triangle, and that's not far from here, you know. Even a whole island disappeared. Maybe that structure was part of it."

"You're mixing up different legends," Claire said with a wave of her hand. "The island you're talking about is Atlantis. It was just a myth. And most of the disappearances in the Bermuda Triangle can be explained anyway. There's always a logical answer if you look for it instead of believing in silly stories."

"OK, Miss Know-it-all," Andrea demanded angrily. "Then what *is* that thing down there?"

Claire shook her head, still smiling. "I don't know. But if

it was anything important, don't you think other people would have explored it by now? Or at least reported it?"

"Maybe they tried," Brandon replied ominously. "And maybe something stopped them."

"Well," Claire said, standing. "I really don't care what it is or why it—Oh, no!" She held up her hand. "My ring! It's gone!" She glanced out toward the water and back to her brother and sister. "I've got to go and look for it."

"You're crazy," Brandon protested. "There's no way you can find a little ring out there."

"I remember where I was swimming the last time I saw it. I can find it if you guys help me," she begged.

The thought of going back into the water scared Andrea, but Claire had already made her feel foolish about her fear. "OK," she agreed reluctantly. "But let's hurry."

With Claire in the lead, the three carefully retraced her path. They had almost given up the search when Brandon suddenly signaled and pointed to something caught on a piece of coral at the edge of the drop-off. It was the ring. Andrea watched Claire dive toward it, but just as her sister reached out to grab the ring, Andrea felt herself heading downward too, against her will. The current had suddenly begun shifting strongly seaward, and even though she kicked as hard as she could, Andrea was swept helplessly toward the drop-off. She lost sight of Brandon altogether, but she saw Claire grabbing at the coral in panic as the unnatural current caught her in its grip as well. It was dragging them over the edge and into the depths . . . right toward the unearthly structure.

Her body screaming for a fresh breath, Andrea felt

consciousness slipping away. She barely noticed as an opening suddenly appeared at the base. Then in a flash, she and her sister and brother were sucked through the gaping maw.

Regaining her senses, Andrea found herself on the stone floor of a gloomy, air-filled chamber with corridors leading off in several directions. Small crystals embedded in the stone walls appeared to be giving off a faint glow.

"Claire!" she cried out. "Brandon!"

"Shhhhhh," her sister hushed her. "We're right here. But you've got to be quiet." There was a tremor in her voice. "I don't think we're alone."

Andrea fell silent and listened to the sound of water falling drop by drop from the roof of the chamber. And yes, there was a shuffling noise, as if something had just moved quickly across the floor of a nearby corridor.

"What are we going to do?" she whispered, pressing closer to her brother and struggling to hold back her tears.

"We have to find a way back to the surface," he answered, trying to sound brave. "One of these corridors may lead upward."

"But even if it does," Andrea moaned, "It might take us farther out to sea."

"We have to take that chance," Claire insisted.

Slowly the three entered the nearest corridor. Andrea's eyes had adjusted to the gloom, enough so that she could make out some mystical carvings on the walls. Whatever they were in, it was clearly no natural formation. But who had built it? And where were they now?

Claire stopped and turned, peering into the shadows

behind her. "I can't shake the feeling that we're being followed," she murmured under her breath.

Andrea felt it too. *It's waiting,* she thought in horror.

The corridor took a turn and ended abruptly. There were entrances to two others, one leading left, the other to the right.

"Let's try this way," Brandon urged, nudging Andrea and Claire to the left. "The other one is going down."

Within a few yards the corridor opened onto a small alcove. Brandon held up his hand for his sisters to wait, and he stepped cautiously inside.

"There's no way out through here," he called back softly. "There's just a lot of piles of stuff . . . they look like big round shells or something. I can't make out what . . ."

Just then Brandon's foot kicked an object at the bottom of one of the piles. Andrea watched as something pale and fairly round rolled toward her feet. She bent down to pick it up, then looked into two empty eyes and a fleshless grin. With a bloodcurdling scream, she dropped it.

"It's a skull!" she sobbed. "A human skull!"

The unstable pile suddenly gave way, and dozens of skulls tumbled across the stone floor.

"Let's get out of here!" Claire yelled, and they dashed back along the corridor that headed down, deeper into the sea bed. Gasping for breath, they finally stumbled into a huge, open chamber and stopped abruptly as if they had been glued to the spot.

Dozens and dozens of dark, cloaked figures stood waiting in the shadows all around them.

Brandon was the first to find his voice. "Who are you?" he murmured hoarsely. "What do you want from us?"

One figure stepped into the dim glow of a crystal and lowered the hood of its cloak. Andrea felt her heart pumping furiously. The being was ghostly pale and slender, with cruel, blood-red eyes.

It opened its mouth to speak and exposed a pair of sharp, gruesome fangs. "Why, child, we want your blood, of course."

"Vampires!" Claire whispered in fright. "But this isn't possible. You don't exist!"

"I assure you we do," the creature said and laughed evilly. "And we have prospered far better than our land-dwelling brethren since we left the surface centuries ago to establish this colony. Here, we are safe from those who would hunt us, *and* from the wretched effects of your miserable sun."

Licking its lips, the hideous vampire moved closer. Andrea glanced back down the corridor, hoping to find an avenue of escape, but saw three shadowy beings barring the way.

"And we have had no shortage of prey. We feed on those of you who are careless enough to stray too close to our realm," the creature gloated. "I imagine the disappearances have caused some alarm, but humans will always seek logical answers—just as they will explain away *your* disappearance, my unfortunate ones."

With that, the grotesque creatures threw back their hoods and, snarling, slowly advanced toward Andrea, Claire, and Brandon. Andrea wanted to run . . . to scream . . . but all she could do was gaze at the horrible face that bore down on her, drowning in the depths of its blood-red eyes.

Air Waves

aron's dad walked purposefully to the television set and shut it off. "Is your homework done?" he asked in an irritated tone.

"Almost," Aaron answered, hedging around the truth, which was that he hadn't even started it yet. "I'll finish it right after this show."

"You'll finish it *now*," his dad demanded. "I'm not going to stand by and watch you turn into a couch potato."

Oh no, Aaron thought. *Here it comes again.*

"I don't see why you want to spend all your time sitting in front of a television, anyway. Why don't you get outside more? Why don't you spend more time with your friends?"

"All my friends watch TV too, Dad," Aaron offered.

His father shook his head and sighed. "You know, when I was a boy . . ." he began.

Aaron pushed his glasses back up onto the bridge of his nose and flopped against the couch cushions. He was trapped. There was nothing he could do now but listen.

"Television was something special that I got to watch *occasionally*," his dad went on. "I spent time with my friends playing baseball or just goofing around."

"I don't like baseball," Aaron said uncooperatively. "Besides, I don't see what the big deal is," he added, knowing that what he was about to say would annoy his father. "Mom never minded when I watched TV. And you never used to complain about it when she was here."

Aaron knew he was standing on firm ground with this statement. Before his parents' divorce, his dad *hadn't* paid much attention to him. Now he was always on his case.

"Well, things are different now," his father replied softly.

"Look," he finally said. "I don't want to fight with you about this all the time. Maybe we can work out a compromise. But for now I want you to finish your homework."

"But Dad," Aaron protested. "It's Friday. I can finish it over the weekend. There's a new sci-fi show starting tonight—*Gamma Brigade*. Everybody's going to watch it."

"Upstairs," his father said, pointing toward Aaron's room.

• • • • • • • • • • •

When Aaron got on the school bus the next Monday morning, everyone was talking about *Gamma Brigade*.

"What did you think of that gamma ray retro-blaster the captain had?" Aaron's friend Eddie asked, sliding into his seat.

"I didn't see it," Aaron answered glumly.

Eddie gaped at him in surprise. "What do you mean? How could you miss it?"

Aaron scowled. "Well, my dad wouldn't let me watch TV," he explained.

Eddie shrugged. "My mom gets like that about TV sometimes. She says that if I watch too much it'll hurt my eyes. But I guess that wouldn't be a problem for you." He grinned and tapped one of the unusually thick lenses of Aaron's special prescription glasses that he wore to correct a bad stigmatism. "You're already blind as a bat."

Aaron smiled back mischievously. "Yeah, I may need glasses, but at least my feet touch the floor when I sit down, Shortie." He and Eddie always poked fun at each other, but they both knew that it was only friendly kidding.

Once he got to school, it was clear to Aaron that he was probably the only kid who had missed the premiere of *Gamma Brigade*.

"So, who thinks the captain is kind of cute?" Becky asked as she joined Aaron and several other kids in the cafeteria at lunchtime.

"I think the dispatcher is more your type," Anne said smugly. Everyone laughed except Aaron.

"What's so funny?" he asked.

"The dispatcher is this really disgustingly ugly alien

dude who hosts the show," Eddie explained. "He's supposed to be able to keep in contact with the characters through their special communicator badges.

"I already sent away for mine."

"Me, too," Becky said, and then she turned to Aaron. "The badges are some kind of promotion. You can get them free if you write to the television station."

Aaron nodded, wondering if he'd ever get to see the show himself.

After dinner the following Friday night, Aaron sat expectantly in front of the TV set. *Gamma Brigade* would be starting in a few minutes, and he and his dad had worked out a deal in which he could watch an hour of TV each night, as long as his homework was finished beforehand. Leaning back, he prepared to become completely lost in what his friends had claimed was the best sci-fi show ever. But as the minutes passed, his disappointment grew.

"What is everybody making such a big deal about?" he muttered when the show was nearly half over. True, the dispatcher was a pretty cool alien. He looked something like a huge, lime-green lizard in a military uniform. But the show itself was hokey. Nevertheless, Aaron followed the instructions given after the credits to obtain his own communicator badge. He printed his name, age, address, and the number of people in his family on a three-by-five card, then mailed it to the TV station.

On the bus the following Monday, Aaron related his disappointment about *Gamma Brigade* to Eddie. "The sets were so cheesy looking!" he said critically. "And even *I* could have written a better story."

"I doubt that," Eddie responded with obvious displeasure. He nonchalantly ran one finger over the communicator badge that he now wore on his shirt at all times. "You're crazy! The show is great."

"What's bothering you?" Aaron asked. "It's only a stupid television show. I just don't think it measures up."

"Measures up? Was that supposed to be some kind of crack about my height?" Eddie demanded angrily.

Aaron couldn't believe that his friend was so upset. "No, I wasn't trying to make a joke. I—"

But Eddie cut him off. "Look, I'm sick of your dumb jokes. And I'm sick of you!" With that, he slid out of his seat and moved to the front of the bus.

At school Eddie soon let the other kids know what Aaron had said about *Gamma Brigade*. By lunchtime he was an outcast—everyone seemed to be taking the show so seriously. Then, during gym class, he was stunned to see that even Coach Mortimer was wearing a communicator badge on his sweatshirt.

By the time Aaron got home he was in a terrible mood. His dad was in the family room, but Aaron went straight to his room and didn't come out until dinnertime. When he did come downstairs, he saw that his dad was still in the family room, sitting on the couch.

"Dad?" he murmured. His father said nothing. The room was lit only by the spectral glow of the TV screen. In the bluish light Aaron could see his father was mesmerized by what he was watching.

"Dad?" Aaron tried again. He glanced at the screen and saw the alien face of the dispatcher. "Dad, what are you doing?" Aaron asked, flipping on the overhead light.

His father turned to him and smiled. "I'm watching that show all you kids are talking about," he said. "I've been a little hard on you lately, so I thought it might be nice if I checked it out . . . sort of met you halfway."

Aaron looked at the screen. "But it's not supposed to be on tonight."

His father laughed. "Well, I heard from Al Johnson, who works at the station, that the show's such a big hit they've decided to air it five days a week. And look here," he declared, holding out a small package. "This arrived in the mail for you. Sorry, I opened it."

Aaron threw a puzzled glance at his father and took the already-opened box. Inside was a communicator badge in a protective plastic bag. "But . . . how did it get here so fast? I only sent for it on—"

"That doesn't matter," his dad interrupted. "Let me help you put it on." He grabbed the package and fumbled with the small plastic bag. Aaron noticed that a similar badge was also pinned to his father's shirt.

"Wait a minute!" Aaron said with a growing sense of dread. "Where did you get that?" He pointed to the badge pinned over his father's left shirt pocket.

"It was in the box when I opened it. The station must have sent one for every member of the family," his father said, reaching toward him. "Let's put yours on. Come on now. Let me help you with this."

"No!" Aaron cried out. Trying to push his dad away, his

watch caught on his father's badge, ripping open his shirt. Aaron gasped in horror. The image of the badge was emblazoned in a raised pattern on his dad's bare chest!

Stumbling back, Aaron could hardly believe his eyes. His father lunged at him again with the badge in hand, but Aaron managed to twist away and charged to the front door. He didn't understand exactly what was going on, but he knew for certain that he didn't want one of those badges on him.

"There's nowhere for you to run!" his father screamed, as Aaron raced into the night. "They'll find you!"

Aaron fled until he felt that his lungs would burst. Finally he had to stop. Gulping in the cool evening air, he realized that he was on the main street of town, but it was completely deserted.

"I've got to get to the police station," he moaned aloud, heading for the two-story brick building at the end of the block. As he passed McKelvey's Electronics he was confronted by dozens of TV sets of every size in the huge display window. The dispatcher's hideous lizard face was on every screen.

"Give yourself up!" the image demanded, its eyes boring into Aaron's. "We *will* find you!"

As Aaron reached the police station, he saw an officer stepping out through the door. In terror he realized that the man had a communicator badge displayed prominently on his uniform. Aaron ducked back into the shadows.

"What am I going to do?" he moaned. He had never felt so alone in his life.

•••••••••••

When the first glimmer of dawn showed on the horizon, Aaron made up his mind. *The television station,* he thought. *That's where everything started. Maybe . . . if I could just shut it down.*

Aaron remembered the address where he had sent his order for the communicator badge. It was only a few blocks away, and keeping to the shadows, he made his way toward it.

There was no one around when he got there. He easily found an unlocked window and managed to work his way inside, dropping into a huge, dark room.

Must be the sound stage, he thought as he moved across the empty area. Then all at once a single powerful spotlight

clicked on, creating a pool of white light only a few feet away from where he stood. Aaron shielded his eyes, and at the same time he felt a slight vibration that seemed to emanate from the floor and walls. A distorted voice spoke from somewhere in the surrounding gloom.

"Join us," it whispered.

As Aaron watched, a figure stepped into the pool of light. He recognized the bizarre, alien features of the *Gamma Brigade* dispatcher. "It isn't going to be so bad," the creature said soothingly. "Though it would have been so much easier if you had surrendered your will . . . like the others." The dispatcher moved closer and leaned toward Aaron as if to get a closer look. "This thick glass you wear over your eyes must have somehow interfered with our broadcast."

Aaron reached up to touch his special lenses, still too dumbfounded to speak.

"Well," the being said with an air of satisfaction. "It doesn't matter now. Our goal has been achieved."

"What goal?" Aaron stammered, finding his voice.

"We came here to find suitable laborers to rebuild our planet. You earthlings are easily influenced and will work quite well for us."

From somewhere deep inside, Aaron dredged up the courage to resist. "No!" he screamed. "I will never join you! I'll find others, and we'll stop you!"

"You're welcome to try," the creature answered with a sound that seemed somewhat like a laugh. "But you will fail."

With that, the lights rose. Aaron saw that he was in a huge, circular area. Dozens of small viewing screens flickered on above him, showing the townspeople sitting placidly and uncaring in small cells. His dad was among them. A single large screen showed planet earth falling rapidly away behind them.

"I'm on your ship," Aaron said in quiet shock. "Aren't I?"

"Clever boy," the alien answered, opening its clawed hand. In its palm rested a communicator badge. "Put it on," the creature commanded. "It will be easier that way."

Aaron watched as his beloved planet grew smaller and smaller on the screen. He turned and reached for the badge, then slowly pinned it over his heart.

Dead Letter Office

Mindy watched her dad load a battered, rusty steamer trunk from the flea market into the back of their pickup truck. "I know you've always told me that there's no such thing as junk, Dad," she said, eyeing the trunk. "But this seems pretty close."

Her father slammed the tailgate closed. "On the contrary, young lady. This trunk is a real find—1930s, I'd say. With some work, it will bring a nice price at the store."

Mindy's father was an antiques dealer, and on weekends he and Mindy would spend time together wandering through flea markets and garage sales in search of treasures.

"So where are we going next?" she asked, settling into the passenger seat.

"There's an estate sale over in Lewisville," her dad said as he backed out of the dirt parking lot. "The man who passed away was the postmaster here in Fayette for forty years before he retired. I understand the old guy collected memorabilia from the post office. It might be interesting."

Sure enough, when Mindy and her dad returned home, the pickup was full of stuff from the old postmaster's collection, along with other odds and ends.

"I'll get this steamer trunk," Mindy's dad said, lifting the ancient-looking chest into the storage shed where he kept his new finds. "Would you grab that stack of old postal sacks?"

"Sure, Dad," she answered, climbing into the bed of the pickup, lifting the dozen or so hefty cotton sacks and following her dad into the shed.

Her father placed the trunk down in a dusty corner with a grunt, and Mindy deposited her burden on top of it. Neither of them noticed the envelope that had slipped out from between the sacks and fallen to the floor.

• • • • • • • • • • •

The next day, as she often did, Mindy gave her friend Chelsea a guided tour through her father's acquisitions. Standing in the storage shed, rummaging through a box of old photos in antique silver frames, Mindy was just commenting on how weird people dressed in the early 1900s when the frame she was holding slipped from her hand and fell to the floor. She leaned down to get it, then noticed an envelope, half hidden behind another box.

"What's this?" she murmured, picking it up.

"It looks like an old letter," Chelsea said uninterested.

Mindy examined the front of the envelope, then turned it over. "That's weird," she observed. "According to the postmark, this is more than forty years old, but it's never been opened." She held the envelope up to the light. "There's a letter inside. Maybe it just got stuck in between a couple of sacks of mail and was never delivered."

"Where was it sent?" Chelsea asked, her curiosity growing. "Maybe we could actually take it there. Wouldn't that be wild? We might even get our pictures in the paper for seeing that a forty-year-old letter was finally delivered!"

Mindy studied the address written in faded blue ink. The handwriting was small and ornate, making it difficult to read. "It's addressed to Miss Carmela Barnes at 553 Oakdale Avenue here in Fayette."

Chelsea shrugged. "So much for that. There aren't any homes on Oakdale Avenue anymore. That part of town is all stores and businesses now."

"Well," Mindy said with a grin. "Then I guess it's OK to open it." Ripping the envelope, she unfolded a single sheet of paper. "This handwriting is the worst!" she exclaimed.

"What does it say?" Chelsea pressed, leaning over her friend's shoulder to see the letter.

"Wow!" Mindy's eyes widened. "Listen to this: 'My dearest Carmela. The crime is done. But knowing that we can now spend our lives together makes everything all right. . . . ' " She paused. "Hmmm, I can't really make this line out," she said, squinting at the small script. "Anyway, this is the important part: 'It won't be too much longer and we will have everything we've ever wanted. As we planned, I'll have to go away for a while until I am sure there is no suspicion. I've hidden the booty in the house where no one else could ever find it.' " Mindy looked at her friend, whose eyes were now as wide as hers. "Then it says something about the fireplace, and it's just signed with the letter *D*."

Chelsea looked confused. "What's booty?" she asked.

"Money!" Mindy declared. "Or something valuable. Don't you get it? Whoever wrote this letter stole something and hid it in his house. Who knows? Maybe it's still there."

"No way," Chelsea said shaking her head, "if this really is true. I'll bet old *D* spent the 'booty' a long time ago."

"Maybe . . . maybe not," Mindy answered with an impish grin. "It's like an old mystery, and I think we should try to solve it. This return address isn't far from here," she said excitedly. "Let's check it out."

It was only a fifteen-minute bike ride to the address that was written in the upper left corner of the old envelope. The girls stood on the sidewalk in front of 427 Broadmore Lane, which turned out to be a dilapidated home.

"How nice," Chelsea said sarcastically. "If the guy really did steal a lot of money, he sure didn't use any of it to fix this place up."

Though it might have once been a fine home, the two-story house appeared as if it hadn't been painted in decades. The shutters were closed, except for one that dangled from an upstairs window, and the roof sagged all over. Mindy leaned her bike against the fence and tugged open the gate.

The hinges squealed as if they were in pain.

"Can I help you girls?" an elderly neighbor woman called from across the street.

Mindy stopped and turned to the woman who approached. "We're trying to find out about the man who owned this place," she answered, half-lying. "My dad buys and sells antiques, and I think we have something that once belonged to him."

"Several people have rented the place," the neighbor replied. "But the owner is a woman. She lives back in Connecticut. I keep an eye on the house for her."

Mindy tried again. "He would have lived here back around 1955." And his name started with a D."

"Oh, you mean Daniel Matheson," the elderly woman responded without hesitation. "Yes, he did once own this house. But he died in a train crash back in '55."

"Oh, how terrible," Mindy said, casting a meaningful glance at Chelsea.

"Sad really . . . and kind of bizarre," the woman continued. "You see, his parents died in a *car* crash. Anyway, they left the estate to his older sister, who wound up running off with some salesman. Of course the house then went to Daniel, but he was so upset about everything that had happened, he closed it up and went away for several months. That's when the train wreck happened, so the house went to his cousin Mildred." The woman shrugged. "She's never even come out to look at it. After the estate was settled Mildred tried to sell it, but no one has ever been interested. The place has a funny feel to it. Some houses have that, you know." She gazed up at the shuttered windows and rubbed her arms as if she felt a chill. "Can't keep the place rented either . . . not for long anyway. Every tenant left suddenly without giving any explanation."

"I wonder why?" Mindy mused, staring at the house.

"Well, one couple claimed to hear strange noises late at night," the woman replied. "But that's all they'd say."

Mindy tugged Chelsea's shirtsleeve. "We have to be going, right, Chelsea?"

"Uh, yeah," Chelsea agreed. "Thank you."

"I hope I was of some help," the woman said, smiling.

"Oh, you were," Mindy replied. "You *definitely* were."

Once the girls had ridden around the corner, Mindy pulled her bike to the side of the road and stopped. Chelsea pulled up alongside her.

"I have a plan," Mindy announced. "We're going to leave our bikes here behind the hedge, sneak back to the house, and take a look around."

"Why?" Chelsea asked. "It looks abandoned."

"Because whatever Daniel Matheson hid is still in there," Mindy said with excitement. "Think about it—he said in the letter he was going away. That's probably when he got killed. We also know that his girlfriend never got the letter, which means she never found out about the money!"

"But if there really is money in there, it's stolen," Chelsea pointed out. "Maybe we should just go to the police."

"No," Mindy objected. "Whoever it was stolen from probably doesn't even think about it anymore. It's like buried treasure. *We* discovered the letter with the clue in it, so whatever we find *we* should be able to keep."

Not entirely convinced, Chelsea agreed to at least check

it out, and together the two girls made their way back to the house, keeping close to the hedge so as not to be seen. Then they slipped over the low fence and began to search for a way into the old place.

"Here," Mindy finally whispered as she tugged on the cellar doors. "There's a rusty old lock, but the wood around it is rotted. I think I can—" With a dull groan, the wood around the lock gave way and the ancient doors fell open. Peering down at a rickety wooden staircase that disappeared into the shadowy cellar, the girls were silent for a moment. Then Chelsea mumbled nervously, "You first."

Mindy nodded gravely, rummaged through the pocket of her jeans, and pulled out the penlight that she kept on her key ring. Carefully she eased down the creaking stairs to the bare stone floor below, and Chelsea followed.

The cellar was dark, and the air felt thick and clammy. The only sound was a slow, steady drip of water. Mindy moved the beam of her penlight from one side to the other and found a wide patch of wall and ceiling that were badly waterstained and covered with a thick growth of mildew. A droplet of water formed on the ceiling and fell into a murky puddle that covered nearly the whole floor.

"Oh, great," Mindy grumbled. "We're going to have to walk through that."

Chelsea shrugged. "Come on. If we're going to do this, let's get it over with."

The girls trod cautiously across the slick floor, their sneakers making squishy sounds in the muck. They had almost made it to the stairs on the opposite side of the room when Mindy felt her feet slipping out from under her. She reached out wildly, grabbed the rough banister, and pulled herself forward, falling to her knees on a lower step.

Suddenly something let out a harsh squeal, leapt onto her pant leg, then dropped into the puddle. Mindy gasped, then turned her penlight just in time to see a huge rat racing toward a hole in the far wall. "Gross!" she screeched.

"Let's get out of here!" Chelsea cried.

"No," Mindy protested, pulling herself back to her feet. "Look." She lit the area at the top of the stairs. The door to the first floor stood open as if inviting them to come up. "I want to see what's inside this place."

Chelsea sighed and followed Mindy to the main floor. It was gloomy and grim, but a little daylight slipped through gaps in the closed shutters, making patterns of light on the walls. The girls stopped at the threshold. The floor was thick with dust, and long-abandoned spiderwebs hung eerily in every corner. The silence was so pronounced that Mindy could almost hear the sound of her own heart beating.

She took a step onto the wooden floor, then another until she reached the center of the room. *It knows we're here,* she thought, trying to fight the sensation that the house *itself* was watching them. She remembered the elderly neighbor woman's comment that the house had a funny feel to it.

"It sure is creepy in here," Chelsea whispered as if reading her thoughts.

Mindy looked around slowly, then pulled the letter from her pocket and studied the poor script once more. "The fireplace," she said at last. "There was something in the letter about the fireplace." She looked at the opposite wall and saw a carved wooden mantle. Below was an oversized opening lined with flame-blackened fire tiles.

The girls stepped closer to the barren fireplace, and Mindy shined her light inside. It was large and deep enough for someone to actually fit inside if they crouched down. Grimacing, Mindy swiped away the cobwebs with the letter, then crawled in.

"I don't see anything," she said, then stopped. The thin fire tiles on the inner left wall of the fireplace weren't covered with soot. In fact, they had fallen away in one corner.

"There's something behind here!" she yelled excitedly. Gripping the broken edge of one of the tiles, she easily pulled it loose.

"What is it?" Chelsea asked, squeezing an arm in and helping Mindy pull away the tiles.

Soon the girls had exposed a small, rough wooden door locked shut with a metal hook. Mindy pried at the hook and it finally popped open. Then for an instant she thought she heard a rustling noise, as if something on the other side had moved back, away from the door.

"What was that?" she murmured.

"What was what?" Chelsea looked at her uneasily

Mindy reached up and pushed at the corner of the door. The rusted hinges resisted for a moment, then screeched open. Shining her light inside what appeared to be a brick chamber about the size of a walk-in closet, Mindy felt her courage draining away. Even though the prize that they were searching for was probably only a few feet away, she was now filled with apprehension.

"Do you think there are rats in there?" Chelsea said with a moan. "It smells awful."

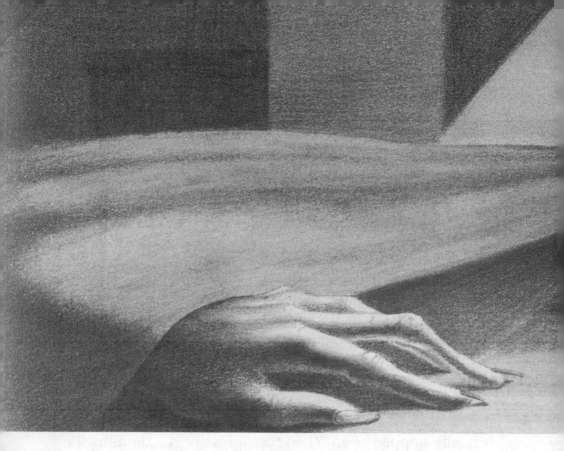

"I—I don't know," Mindy stammered. Gathering her nerve she inched forward. "Let's just take a quick look," she said, as much to reassure herself as to comfort her friend.

Once through the low door, Mindy stood still clutching the letter. Chelsea wriggled through as well, and the two huddled close together as Mindy moved her light around the small room.

"Look!" Chelsea cried, pointing to something hidden under a blanket in the corner. "That's it! That's the booty!"

Mindy smiled uncertainly and stepped toward the long, dark object. She reached out her hand, then stopped and drew back a little. Something wasn't right.

"Go ahead," Chelsea urged.

Once again Mindy touched the edge of the blanket, then slowly—very, very slowly—she pulled it back.

Without warning a pale, lifeless hand darted out from under the blanket and gripped Mindy's wrist. A scream of horror rose in her throat and she struggled like a trapped animal to pull away. But whatever had her in its grasp held her with tremendous power.

"Mindy!" Chelsea shrieked, unable to see what had struck such terror in her friend. "What's going on?"

Just then the putrid blanket fell away, and both girls could see the loathsome creature that it had hidden. Slowly a skeletal being rose from the shadows as Mindy and Chelsea cringed and backed away in abject fear.

The creature's head was little more than a skull, with a brittle cascade of what was once long, blond hair. It opened its mouth and rasped in a dry, unearthly voice, "I have waited for so long for that door to be opened. From the moment I awoke to find my murderous brother sealing me alive in this cursed tomb I have refused, by my will alone, to accept death. And now—"

"Run!" screamed Mindy. But just as the girls lunged toward the open door, it swung shut and the metal latch fell closed.

"No!" Chelsea screamed, throwing herself at the door.

"Oh, yes!" The hideous cadaver threw back its head and shuddered with demented laughter. "Now you are both trapped with me. Don't you think I screamed and pounded on that door? But no one heard me, and no one will hear you." The terrible creature cackled. "It seems that it is my fate to remain here, but at least I will no longer be alone."

"Do something!" Chelsea wailed to Mindy as she struggled to open the door. "Help me!"

Hot tears rolled from Mindy's eyes, but she didn't move. In the dull glow from her penlight, she could see the remains of blood-stained scratches where someone else had once tried to claw her way to freedom. She could also see something else. The letter had fallen open to the floor and she was able to read the last few lines again. Then something inside of her mind snapped and she too began to laugh insanely, not unlike the crazed cadaver. It wasn't the booty that Daniel Matheson had hidden before he left that home, never to return . . . it was the *body*.

The Wrath of Pele

Tendrils of wispy steam rose here and there from the sunken landscape that was the summit of Kilauea, one of the active volcanoes on the island of Hawaii.

"It looks more like the surface of the moon than part of a tropical island," David's dad commented as the family took in the view from the museum at park headquarters.

"Is it gonna blow?" David's younger brother, Chip, asked with some concern.

David shook his head. "Do you think they'd let all of these tourists anywhere near this place if the volcano was going to erupt?" He gestured toward about a dozen people who were also enjoying the view.

"Actually, they would," someone said. David turned to see the speaker, a pleasant-faced young man who appeared to be a native islander. "Kilauea has actually been in a state of eruption since 1983," he informed them. "Sometimes it's more spectacular than others. Pele's been busy."

"What's Pele?" David asked.

The young man smiled. "Not what—who. Pele is the great fire goddess, and her home is there in Halemaumau." He pointed to a distant depression in the floor of the crater. "She's moody and short-tempered, and when she's angry, she stamps her foot so hard the ground quakes." He looked thoughtful for a moment. "But Pele is a builder, too. At times she sends lava to the sea. When the fiery flows harden, they have been known to add hundreds of acres of new land to the island."

"That sounds spectacular," David's mom said, her eyes filled with wonder as she gazed at the volcano.

"It is," the islander responded. "Actually, if you want to get a closer look at the lava reaching the sea, just drive about twenty miles out toward the ocean and see for yourself. But be careful. The water may look calm, but it can be dangerous if you get too close."

"Can we go, Dad? Please," Chip begged.

David looked hopefully at his parents. "It sounds really cool!" he exclaimed. "Maybe I could even find some neat rocks for my collection."

The young islander quickly held up his hand. "Oh, no. Pele is a selfish goddess. It would be disrespectful for a stranger to steal what is hers, and anyone who does will inevitably feel her revenge." His tone grew ominous. "Some say that in retribution Pele claims the offender's spirit as her own to serve her forever, initiating her new slave in a bath of fire." Then the young man winked, making David unsure if the grim tale was meant to be taken seriously or not.

Once back in the rental car, David's mom took a look at the map. "Here it is," she said tracing a line with her finger. "It really isn't that far out of our way."

David's father smiled. "Well then, let's do it."

From the backseat Chip suddenly asked, "People don't really believe that stuff about the fire goddess, do they?"

"I'm sure many do," his mom answered. "These islands have a very rich history and tradition. Besides, we shouldn't just discount something because we don't understand it."

"True," his father added. "But that man at the museum was making the story more dramatic for our benefit. The earthquakes on this island are caused when pressure builds up and is released in the volcanoes, not when some mythological goddess stamps her foot."

After a few miles the highway narrowed and finally became no more than a dirt road. David's dad pulled into an open area that appeared to be a rough parking lot, and everyone got out. All around were signs of past lava flows. Jumbles of black and reddish-brown volcanic rock sloped down to the sea. Here and there, hardy vegetation had gained footholds to form oases of green.

"There's the path!" David yelled, racing ahead.

"Not so fast," his mom called out. She pointed to a sign near the path that said CLOSED TO THE PUBLIC.

"Aw, c'mon," Chip begged. "There's nobody here."

"Who's gonna know if we go a little closer," David insisted. "I really want to get a piece of rock as a souvenir."

Their mom shook her head. "I'm sure they had a good reason for closing the path. Remember what the man at the museum said. This area can be dangerous."

"And as for taking a rock," their dad added sternly, "even if you don't share someone else's beliefs, you really must respect their wishes."

As David walked glumly back to the car, he noticed a glassy black rock no bigger than a walnut on the ground, and since no one was watching, he picked it up. Heavy for its size, the rock felt smooth and warm in his hand. *What can it hurt?* he thought. *We'll be gone by tomorrow.* Slipping the rock into his pocket, David looked up to see Chip staring at him with that you're-not-supposed-to-do-that look in his eye. Knowing Chip liked secrets, David put a finger to his lips, signaling his little brother not to tell.

The next afternoon David sat quietly in a window seat of an airplane that would take him and his family back home.

David was sorry to be leaving, but he was glad he'd come away with his special souvenir. He could feel the shape of the glassy black rock in the pocket of his jeans. He fidgeted in his seat. The rock still felt warm . . . *uncomfortably* warm.

"Are you OK, honey?" his mom asked.

"Yeah," David replied. Below the islands slipped from view, and there was only sparkling blue ocean as far as the eye could see. The unpleasant sensation passed. "I'm fine."

It was very late when the family arrived at the airport in Los Angeles, and past midnight when they got home.

David could barely keep his eyes open while he undressed for bed. As he threw his jeans over the back of a chair, the glassy black rock fell out of his pocket and rolled into the center of the room. Picking it up, he tossed the rock onto his desk, crawled into bed, and fell fast asleep.

•••••••••••

When David awoke it was already nine o'clock. His body was still operating on Hawaii time, where it was only six o'clock. Groggy, David pulled the comforter over his head. Suddenly his eyes popped open. Was something burning?

Slipping out of bed, he traced the source of the smell to a small patch of his desktop that appeared slightly charred. At the center of the marred spot was the volcanic rock.

"This is too weird," David muttered under his breath. He reached out and touched the wooden desktop. It was eerily warm, but the rock itself was cool.

"There's a logical explanation for this," he said aloud. "This kind of rock probably gives off heat for a while." He dumped out all the pencils from a metal box on his desk, slid the rock into the box, and snapped the lid shut. Then he slipped the box into his T-shirt drawer and hurried to get dressed. But as he opened his bedroom door to head downstairs for breakfast, he once again caught a faint whiff of smoke. It was coming from his T-shirt drawer.

Hoping that he was wrong, David pulled open the drawer, then drew back in alarm. The metal tin was glowing, and the T-shirts near it were badly scorched.

Without thinking he reached out for the metal box, then pulled his fingers away in pain. "What am I gonna do?" he moaned. He couldn't ask his parents for help. They would want to know where the rock came from, and he would have to admit that he had disobeyed them. And then he had an idea.

Racing to his closet, David frantically tossed aside a few things, then dragged out his science kit. He yanked open the top and pulled out a pair of metal tongs. Maneuvering carefully, he used the tongs to pry open the metal box. He then clamped them around the glowing rock.

Creeping downstairs, still gripping the rock with the tongs, David pressed himself against the wall to avoid being seen by his parents, who were busily preparing a late breakfast in the kitchen. Sweat trickled down his forehead, but he managed to silently slide the glass patio door open. Once outside he tossed the bizarre rock into the fish pond that his dad had so proudly constructed in one corner of the backyard.

The water sputtered and sizzled a little as the rock slipped beneath the surface, and two or three small goldfish swam close to investigate, then quickly zipped away.

• • • • • • • • • • •

"It's the strangest thing I've ever seen in my life!" David's dad said later that day as he stepped through the patio doors holding a shallow bucket. "The pond is dried up."

David, sitting at the kitchen table working on an airplane model with Chip, snapped his gaze up to his father. A stab of fear made his muscles tighten.

David's mom turned from the counter where she'd been slicing apples to make a pie. "What on earth do you mean?"

"Just what I said," he responded. "It's dry as a bone. This

is all that was left." He opened a newspaper onto the kitchen floor and emptied the contents of the bucket. Several withered fish lay lifeless within a tangled mat of parched water plants. He shook the bucket and a small, glassy black rock slid out.

"Hey, David," Chip began. "That's the rock you—" But David kicked him sharply under the table.

"I just don't understand," their father said in puzzlement. "It hasn't been that hot here, and it should take weeks for the water to evaporate like this. I know I checked the level before we went away." He shook his head. "I suppose I should check to see if there are any leaks."

David's mom carefully put down her paring knife. "Well, I've got to see this for myself," she declared.

"Me, too," Chip added, bounding from his chair.

David looked at the dead fish. "I'll just throw these poor guys in the trash."

As soon as the rest of the family was outside, David bent down, and with trembling fingers, picked up the now cool rock. Clutching it tightly in his fist, he whispered fearfully as if trying to appease some invisible being. "I'm sorry. I didn't mean to make you angry." Then he slipped the rock into his pocket, wrapped the dead fish and plants in the newspaper, and stuffed them into the trash.

The patio door slid open again and everyone trooped into the kitchen.

"It's really weird," Chip announced. "Don't you want to see it, David?"

But before he could answer, his mother put her hand on

his forehead. "Are you OK?" she asked with concern. "You look a little feverish."

"I'm fine," he lied. How could he tell her about the icy dread that was seeping into his thoughts . . . the growing terror that an ancient being half an ocean away was seeking retribution for his thoughtless act?

Throughout the rest of the day, he tried to figure out what to do. Just when it seemed there was no way to get rid of the rock, David had an idea. Going straight to his father's garden shed, he found a small shovel. Then he scooped a shallow hole in the rich, dark soil of the flower garden. With his heart pounding, David fished the rock from his pocket, dropped it into the hole, and quickly covered it up.

"There," he declared. "Now you can't do any harm."

• • • • • • • • • • •

The next night, David's parents went out to dinner, leaving him in charge of taking care of Chip.

"Here's the telephone number of the restaurant where we'll be," his mom said, handing David a piece of notebook paper. "We won't be late. I've told Mrs. Samuels next door that you two will be home alone, and she said she'd be happy to come over if you need anything."

"We'll be fine, Mom," David replied.

With the rock buried in the flower garden now out of his mind, David was confident that he had beaten Pele's wrath. Thirty minutes later he felt the first tremors beneath his feet.

"Did you feel that?" Chip questioned, looking up from the TV screen. "Was it an earthquake?"

"Probably," David responded casually. He was used to the tiny quakes that were common to the Los Angeles area.

Suddenly a stronger tremor shook the house and Chip dove under the sturdy wooden coffee table.

David screamed for his brother to stay put. From his vantage point, he had a clear view of the patio and backyard beyond, and what he saw made his legs buckle: A huge, jagged rift had opened in the flower bed. As the house shook more violently the rift widened, and red flames spewed high into the night sky.

Riveted to the spot, David watched in horror as a tall, slender being rose from within the inferno. Her entire body glowed intensely as if it were white hot, and her long hair flickered and danced like flames.

"Pele!" he managed to choke out.

Her fiery eyes blazed with anger, and she held out her hands to David while the ground continued to vibrate and things tumbled down everywhere.

"No!" he shrieked, as the words of the young man at the museum screamed in his brain. *Some say that in retribution Pele claims the offender's spirit as her own to serve her forever.*

Twisting away, David attempted to run, but a wall of fire sprang up around him, blocking his retreat. Through the blaze, he could see Chip cringing in terror under the coffee table. "Give her the rock back!" he screamed.

"It's too late!" David cried. Then, against his will, he moved helplessly toward the fiery goddess.

Faithful Friends

Seth and Monica each stifled a laugh as Gary slipped quietly onto the darkened, sagging porch of old Eli Cane's run-down farmhouse. The three kids delighted in doing things to cause Eli as much grief as possible. Because the house was isolated, he was an easy target whenever they felt like pulling one of their mean-spirited pranks, which was whenever they had nothing better to do. Last spring they'd ripped out his vegetable patch and poured salt on the ground so nothing else would grow. During the summer they'd poured sugar in the gas tank of his tractor and ruined it. Eli had told the sheriff that he thought they were responsible for the damage, and the sheriff hadn't been surprised. It wasn't the first time the three kids had been accused of such activities. Gary had gotten into trouble with his dad, but no one was able to prove anything.

As far as anyone knew, Eli had no family and had lived alone for as long as he'd lived in Bartholomew County. There weren't any neighbors within a mile of his dilapidated place, and his gruff demeanor kept most everyone away. Eli's only companion, up until last month, had been a dog—a scruffy mongrel that was said to be part wolf. Eli had called her Stitch, and she used to bark and howl whenever anyone would get too near the house. But Stitch had finally died and now the elderly man was really alone. With the mutt gone, it was even easier for Seth, Monica, and Gary to torment Eli Cane, and this time they had something special planned.

Slowly and carefully, Gary eased up to the window and peered inside the elderly man's living room. Then he waved to the others, a silent signal for them to follow him. Carrying several plastic bags filled with garbage collected from the trash bin behind the diner in town, Seth and Monica quickly joined him on the porch.

"He's asleep in front of the fire," Gary whispered excitedly. "Give me one of those bags."

Monica handed one to Gary. He unwound the twist tie that held it closed, then made a face. "Pe-ew, this stuff stinks!" he declared aloud.

"Shut up," Seth growled. "Old Eli will hear you."

"No he won't. He's half deaf," Gary said, grinning evilly. "C'mon, let's have some fun."

Monica and Seth opened the bags they were holding and

the kids began to spread the gooey, smelly garbage outside of Eli's house. Suddenly Seth stopped and motioned for the others to do the same.

"What was that?" he asked hesitantly. "Did you guys hear something?" He turned and looked out toward the woods beyond the barn, but even in the light of the full moon, Seth couldn't see a thing.

Monica listened for a moment, then shook her head. "I didn't hear anything."

"It sounded like a wolf or something," Seth said, his brow furrowed with concern.

"Yeah," Gary snickered. "I'll bet it was old Stitch comin' to get us."

"That's not funny," Seth said solemnly. "We have to go through those woods to get home."

Monica tossed her empty plastic bag into the bushes nearby and scowled. "Seth is right. You shouldn't joke like that—you might make it come true." She lowered her voice as if telling a secret. "My big brother said that no grave would hold that she-wolf when she died. He said Stitch was just plain mean."

"You are so weird," Seth scoffed. "When something is dead, it's dead. Besides, how would your brother know?"

"He thinks Stitch was the one killing the sheep we lost a couple of months ago," Monica replied. "He shot at her as she ran away and he thought he hit her in the right leg, but she just kept going."

Seth shook his head. "Something's been killing sheep in this county for a long time, but it isn't any mangy old dog. They're probably real wolves down from the mountains.

59

Besides," he sneered, "your brother couldn't hit an elephant at twenty feet."

"Oh yeah?" Monica put her hands on her hips. "I'll bet he did get Stitch and that's why she died."

"I'll take that bet," Seth said, offering his hand out in defiance.

"You're on," Monica answered back, shaking his hand and glaring at him.

"I have an idea," Gary said, trying to break the silent standoff. "Let's go see who's right."

"What do you mean?" Monica and Seth asked in unison.

"I know where Old Eli buried Stitch," Gary replied, grinning widely. "I saw him one day standing and talking to a mound of dirt up behind the barn. I'll bet that's her grave. It wouldn't take long to dig her up and see if she has any buckshot in her."

Seth and Monica glanced at each other.

"C'mon," Gary urged. "You're not scared, are you?"

"No," Seth answered, shaking his head. "Let's go get some shovels."

Moments later the three stood in the shadow of the barn facing a large patch of bare dirt. They all clutched shovels they had found in Eli's toolshed.

"Let's do it," Seth said slowly.

"You first," Gary goaded Seth and Monica. "It's *your* bet."

Seth and Monica looked at each other and hesitated.

"Fine," Gary said with a snort as he leaned over and pushed his own shovel deep into the soft soil. Seth and Monica began to dig as well, and it wasn't long before they hit something hard.

"Hold up, you guys," Gary ordered. Using the tip of his shovel, he carefully outlined what looked like a large, rough wooden box. "Let's dig around it so we can get it out."

It took all three of them to clear the dirt away and wrestle the box to the surface, balancing it at the edge of the grave. Exhausted, Monica plopped down next to the box and looked at her friends.

"Now what?" she asked.

Gary's lips curled up in an evil smile. "Now we open it and see what's inside."

As he pried at the edges of the box, a ragged cloud snaked across the face of the moon, sending dark fingers of shadow across the field toward them.

Monica jumped to her feet, shivering. "Wait a minute, Gary. This is spooky," she whispered. "Maybe we shouldn't do this. I mean, what if Stitch really could come . . ."

Just then the door to the toolshed slammed shut in a gust of wind, and Monica's warning caught in her throat. Startled, she jumped and hit the corner of the box. In a shower of dirt, it slipped partly back into the hole and popped open.

All three of the kids stared into the vacant eyes of the decomposing dog. Her lips had been drawn back in death, exposing her long, sharp teeth, looking as if she were snarling.

"Ohhhh!" Monica gasped, as a horrible stench filled the air.

Seth stumbled back. "Let's go," he begged. "I don't like this."

"No, wait!" Gary commanded. He stared for a moment at the body, and then he glanced toward the house. "I've got an idea." And he quickly told the others what he had in mind.

"I don't know about this," Monica said once she had heard the whole plan. "It's too weird."

"Yeah," Seth agreed. "And it sounds kind of risky to me."

"It's just a dead dog," Gary argued. "She can't hurt anybody." To make his point he tossed a pebble into the open box. It hit the dog's body with a dull thud. "It'll be fun. We can really drive Eli crazy. All we have to do is hide the body back in the woods, then coax the old man into coming out and finding the empty grave."

"What makes you think he'll fall for it?" Seth asked.

"That old mutt was the only family Eli ever had. She meant everything to him. If he doesn't believe she's come back from the dead, at least he'll *want* to believe it." He looked at the still, anxious expressions on his friends' faces. "It'll be a real goof. That is," he said looking straight at Monica, "unless you're too chicken."

"I'm not chicken," Monica said slowly, annoyed by the comment. Then she looked up with a cruel, determined glint in her eye. "Let's do it."

Seth shrugged, "I'm in."

After finding a canvas tarp in Eli's shed, the three lifted the body into it.

"This is really gross," Monica grumbled, wrinkling up her nose. "She smells. And she's giving me the creeps. Can't we close her eyes or something? She's looking right at me."

"She'll be covered up in a minute," Gary answered. "Quit complaining."

Seth made a face. "Are you sure she's dead? She doesn't feel dead. I thought bodies were supposed to get stiff."

"That's only for a while," Gary said, throwing him a disgusted look. "She's dead all right."

The trio silently lifted their burden and carried it off into the woods.

Afterward, the three doubled back to the farmhouse. While Monica and Seth crouched in the bushes, Gary sprinted toward the porch. He checked to see that Eli was still asleep, then tapped loudly on the windowpane. The old man stirred.

"*Aaaaaaooooooooooo,*" Gary howled, as Monica and Seth clamped their hands over their mouths to keep from laughing. Inside, Eli sat up straight and listened.

Using a long stick, Gary scratched at the door. "*Aaaaaoooo,*" he howled again, then added in a pitiful whine, "Eeeeeeliiiiiiii." Then he leapt from the edge of the porch and rolled into the bushes just as Eli yanked open the door.

"Stitch!" the aged man called out in a frail voice. "Is that you, girl?!" Wincing and rubbing his right leg as he limped, Eli hobbled down the stairs, across the front yard, and to the site of the now open grave. He stared down at the upturned earth in disbelief.

Keeping to the shadows, the kids moved in close enough to watch the results of their practical joke.

"Please, girl!" Eli suddenly cried out once more. "If you're here, let me see you!" His face was twisted in suffering, and when his pitiful plea faded unanswered into the night, he just stood there for a while with his head in his hands, his shoulders trembling.

"What's he doing?" Seth whispered.

"Shhhhhh!" Monica answered, hitting Seth hard in the arm.

63

Eli suddenly looked up in their direction. Then he raised his head almost as if he were sniffing the breeze.

"Hmmph," he muttered, turning and shuffling toward the house. He stopped once more when he reached his door and looked back toward them.

"You don't think he can see us, do you?" Monica moaned.

"No way," whispered Gary.

"Well, I say we get out of here anyway," Seth urged. "I suddenly have a really creepy feeling about this."

"Maybe we should put the dog back," Monica offered.

"I don't want to go near that thing," said Seth. "Let's just go."

The others agreed, and they took off toward the main road, only about a quarter of a mile through the woods. For a while the kids walked in silence. The tall, dark trees seemed to press toward them, letting in only small splashes of pale moonlight to show the path. Monica was the first to speak.

"Do you guys think . . . I mean, you really don't believe that things can come back after they're dead?"

"Of course not!" Gary said with a sneer. "You've seen too many movies."

The girl pulled her jacket more tightly around her shoulders and whimpered, "I don't like this. I feel like we're being watched." She looked from side to side. "I keep seeing that dog's eyes looking right at me."

They walked a little farther, but now it seemed as if there was something different in the woods . . . something sinister.

"Stop," Seth said abruptly. "What was that?"

Gary let out a groan. "Oh, great. Now you're hearing things again. I didn't hear—"

"Shut up!" Seth demanded, holding up his hand. He peered into the darkness around them.

"I heard something, too," Monica murmured after a moment. It came from back there." She pointed in the direction they had come from.

They all stood perfectly still and listened to the gentle breeze sighing softly in the treetops. Suddenly an owl hooted in the distance, followed by something else. As they strained to hear what it was, a low rumbling noise sounded behind a tangle of branches just a few feet away.

Monica tried to catch her breath. "There's something there!" she gasped. In answer, the branches began to crackle and snap. Then, with a deep, guttural roar, a huge shadowy form sprang from the gloom. Gary let out a piercing cry and charged headlong down the path with Monica at his heels. Somewhere behind them Seth's horrible screams ripped through the night.

As Gary lurched forward along the path, sharp branches reached out and tore at his face. His breath came in ragged gulps that stung his chest. Then all at once he stumbled and fell hard on the cold ground. Something tumbled on top of him and he screeched in terror.

"It's me!" Monica cried hysterically. "What are we going to do? It already got Seth and it's coming after us! We've got to get out of here!"

Gary scrambled to his feet and pulled the hysterical girl up behind him.

"This way," he commanded. "The road is just up ahead."

But as they turned to run, a ghastly figure crashed through the undergrowth and leaped into their path. Gary was frozen to the spot, his heart about to burst. Crouched

right in front of him was some sort of hideous, wolflike beast. It was covered with stiff, rust-colored fur, and it glared at them with flaming, blood-red eyes. Droplets of foam dripped from its razor-toothed jaws.

"It must be the spirit of Stitch!" Gary heard Monica scream beside him. "She's come back as a ghost because of what we did to her body and to the old man."

Slowly, with a tremendous effort, Gary managed to force himself to move. He inched away, a little at a time. Just as slowly, the phantom creature began to slink toward them.

Monica reached out and brushed at Gary's hand.

"Don't leave me," she begged.

Gary pulled his hand away, and with a sudden surge of strength, he took off running. Monica's shrieks filled his ears, but he didn't even look back. He knew what he had to do. He raced to the spot where they had left the tarp-covered body of the terrible dog. If the thing really was a vengeful spirit after them because of what they had done, then maybe it would leave him alone if he buried the body again.

With tears streaming down his face, Gary dragged the body across the field. *I can do this,* he tried to convince himself. *I've got to do this.*

The pallid moon shone down on him as he worked feverishly to place the corpse back into the box and rebury it.

Finally he let the shovel fall from his sweating hands. It was done. "There," he said aloud as if the spirit dog could hear him. "That's what you wanted, isn't it? Now leave me alone." Covered with dirt, Gary backed slowly away from the grave . . . and bumped into something. Slowly he turned around and came face to face with Eli.

"You!" Gary screamed wildly. "It's all your fault!"

The man looked at him without emotion.

"Seth is dead, and Monica is probably dead, too," Gary yelled. "I'm going to tell everyone that you and your monster dog are murderers!"

Eli simply shook his head. "You're wrong, boy. So very wrong," he whispered as he glanced down at the grave. "She's no monster. All that's buried here are the earthly remains of a dog . . . a gentle, faithful old friend who accepted me for what I really am." He looked up. "Stitch was my only friend. You should never have disturbed her resting place. You should never have tried to hurt me by defiling her grave." He paused for a moment. "You've done harm to me before, and I've let it pass as just spiteful pranks, but this time you've mistreated my friend. This time I will not let it go unpunished."

Gary felt his tortured heart begin to pound again as the man's eyes began to glow a fiery red, the same crimson color as those of the beast that attacked him and Monica. Numbed by fear, he could barely breathe.

"You're wrong about something else, too," Eli snarled. The bright moonlight illuminated the stiff, rust-colored hairs now protruding from his changing shape. "And you were wrong about telling everyone about me." Saliva streamed from the corner of Eli's mouth as his teeth grew sharp and gleaming white. His jaws extended into a long, wolfish snout. His transformation to werewolf complete, Eli moved ominously toward his victim. "You were wrong . . . because you aren't going to be around to tell anybody . . . anything."

Bungalow 14

he sign at the edge of the highway read NO FACILITIES NEXT 100 MILES.

"There's a gas station just up ahead," Stephen's dad pointed out. "We'd better stop and fill the tank." He turned the family van off the road and eased it next to a bank of gas pumps in the shade of the station overhang.

Stephen's mom opened the passenger door, then turned in her seat to face him and his older sister, Liz. "I'm going to use the rest room, and I think you two had better do the same. It looks like we won't be able to find a motel until we get closer to Albuquerque."

"Oh great," Liz grumbled. "Just what I wanted to hear—

I get to spend another two hours cooped up in the backseat with my darling brother."

"Well excuse me for living, your highness," Stephen shot back.

"Please!" their mom said, rubbing her forehead with her fingertips. "None of us wants to spend any more time on the road then we have to, so let's just try to make the best of it." She slid out of her seat and slammed her door.

"Great work," Liz complained, frowning at her brother as she, too, got out of the van.

"Me?" he protested. "You started it. Why do I get blamed for everything?"

Stephen hopped out and slid the door closed. Feeling for change in the pockets of his jeans, he scooped out a couple of quarters. He bought an icy cold soda from the station vending machine, then walked to where the blacktop of the gas station bordered on the endless expanse of desert beyond. Shading his eyes, Stephen looked toward the far-off mountains, wondering what sort of secrets they might hold. The landscape in between was mile upon mile of pale sand, dotted with dried brush. A black ribbon of highway sliced through it. In the distance, the road appeared to be flooded by a lake of rippling blue water, but Stephen knew it was only an illusion—a mirage caused by the unrelenting heat. He felt the sunbaked ground sizzle beneath the soles of his sneakers.

Kicking a pebble into a knot of parched brush a few feet away, he froze. From within the meager shade of the brush came a dry, rattling sound, followed by a swift movement. Stephen recognized the long, slender body of a rattlesnake. The startled creature drew itself back in a tight S-curve with its triangular-shaped head lifted in defense above the sand. Stephen knew that the head was shaped to accommodate deadly venom glands. He also knew not to do anything that would alarm the animal more than he already had. Rigid with fear, his head pounding, Stephen waited until the rattlesnake silently withdrew.

"Whoa," he gasped, and retreated to the safety of the van. "Dad!" he yelled. "You won't believe this!"

His father was talking to the station attendant and held up one hand to quiet his son. With a sigh, Stephen climbed back into the vehicle. His sister was reading a magazine. "Liz," he said excitedly, "I just saw a rattlesnake! It was only a few feet away."

"Good thing it didn't bite you," she said with a nasty grin. "It might have gotten sick."

Stephen scowled. "Yeah? Well, I scared it away by showing it a picture of you."

"That's enough, you two," Stephen's dad ordered as he got back into the driver's seat. "The attendant told me that there's a small motel just off the main road a couple of miles from here. It isn't fancy, but he said they always have vacancies. What do you say we stop there for the night and get some rest? It might improve everybody's mood."

"That's a great idea," Stephen's mom said with a smile. "As long as the room has a shower and a bed, it's fancy enough for me."

The turnoff wasn't far, and a few minutes later they pulled into a dusty parking area. A sun-bleached red pickup truck was parked in front of one of the rooms. The motel was made up of three single-story adobe buildings painted the same lifeless color as the surrounding sand. The units were arranged around a central court with a swimming pool that was empty, aside from some tumbleweeds.

"The attendant didn't exaggerate about it not being fancy," Stephen's mom commented. "But it's better than nothing. Let's go see about getting a couple of rooms."

The door to the small motel office was open, but there was no one at the desk. "Anybody here?" Stephen's dad called out. Then, noticing a bell on the counter, he tapped it several times.

A door opened at the rear of the room and a tall, slim man in jeans, a faded denim shirt, and a cowboy hat stepped inside. Stephen noticed that his well-worn boots appeared to be made of snakeskin, but it was what the man wore around his neck that really drew his attention. Hanging from a short strip of leather was the skull of a rattlesnake with its ivory white fangs exposed as if ready to strike.

"What do you folks want?" the man asked in an unfriendly tone.

"A couple of rooms," Stephen's dad answered. "Just for tonight."

"I don't think I have anything right now," the man stated flatly.

Stephen's dad looked surprised. He motioned to a board behind the desk that contained fourteen hooks. A key hung from each of them except the last two. "But it doesn't look like everything has been rented. I don't understand."

The surly man folded his arms and leaned across the registration desk. "We're doing some . . . renovations," he replied. "Most of the rooms are unavailable. You're better off driving into Albuquerque."

"Look," Stephen's dad said firmly. "My family is very tired. I don't know what the problem is, but we're willing to take just about anything. Can't we at least *see* the rooms?"

"Of course you can," someone said from behind them. Stephen turned to see a tall woman standing in the doorway. He couldn't help but stare at her strange, yellowish eyes. They were almost hypnotic. "Sam," she said in a scolding manner, "don't be so unneighborly. Bungalows 5 and 6 are all freshly made up. I'm sure these folks will be just fine in there."

The man seemed suddenly nervous . . . perhaps even frightened. "I think . . . we have enough guests for tonight," he offered hesitantly.

"Sam!" the woman said with a trace of irritation, her eyes glittering. "Fortune has provided us with more. We really must get them settled before dark."

With surprise, Stephen thought he saw the skull that hung around the man's neck move slightly. Sam's eyes appeared to glaze over momentarily. The man shuddered, then reached for two keys. "Suit yourselves," he grumbled, handing them to Stephen's dad.

"That guy is really weird," Stephen declared once he and his sister were in their room munching on sandwiches his mom had supplied from the cooler in the van. He popped the last bite of his sandwich into his mouth. "Hey, you want to check this place out?" he asked, his mouth full. "It's still light enough."

"No thanks," Liz answered as she flopped onto one of the twin beds. "You can be Mr. Explorer if you want. I'm too tired."

"You're such a drag," Stephen griped, heading for the

door. "Tell Mom and Dad I'll be back in a few minutes." Once outside, he examined the empty pool and parking area, and began to explore a shallow ditch near the roadway. From his vantage point he had a clear view of the entire motel. He watched as the strange woman he had met earlier left the office and strode purposefully toward the last bungalow. The sun was just beginning to set behind the mountains, streaking the sky with red and orange, but even in the failing light he could make out two or three slender, sinuous shadows on the ground that seemed to be keeping pace with her.

"Are those snakes?" he asked aloud. *Nah, even pet snakes don't follow people around,* he thought. *It must be a trick of the light.*

The woman looked up toward the darkening sky with an odd smile that even from a distance gave Stephen an uncomfortable feeling. Then she hurriedly entered the bungalow.

A soft, cooling breeze began to sigh across the desert. Stephen trotted back toward the building, then prowled along the cracked concrete walkway that ran the length of the motel, stopping to peek into the front window of each room.

"They don't look like they're being renovated to me," he muttered. In bungalow 13 he saw an older man stretched out across one of the beds. He appeared to be sound asleep. A half-empty liquor bottle stood on the nightstand.

The last room was bungalow 14. Unlike the others, the drapes were pulled tightly across the unlit window, kindling Stephen's curiosity. He crept up to the door and carefully tried the knob, but it was locked. He put his ear to the door.

At first everything seemed quiet, but as the last rays of the sun disappeared, he thought he heard something stir inside. There was a slight rattling noise that sent a chill down his spine. Suddenly a door slammed at the motel office, and he scurried back to his room.

"Now what?" Liz complained as Stephen raced into his motel room, locked the door, closed the drapes, and peeked out like a fugitive. "Have you done something to get in trouble again?"

"Shhhh!" Stephen hissed. "I'll tell you in a minute." Still breathing hard, he watched as the thin man from the front desk, Sam, strode purposefully to bungalow 13 and went inside. He came out again, holding up the elderly man Stephen had seen there earlier. Together the two shuffled toward bungalow 14. Sam fumbled for the key, opened the door, and guided the old man inside.

After a few minutes Sam reappeared alone. He stopped, leaned against the wall, and put his face in his hands. Then he walked slowly back to the office. Seconds later the garish orange neon vacancy sign flared to life.

Stephen turned to his sister. "There's something strange going on here," he said. "Something *very* strange."

"*You're* strange," Liz said sleepily. "Turn out the light, will you? I'm exhausted."

Stephen flipped off the overhead light and sat for a while in darkness, watching to see if anything more happened in bungalow 14, but there was nothing. Finally he stretched out on his own bed and fell into a restless sleep.

In his dream, Stephen found himself alone at night, in the middle of the desert. He called for his parents, but the only answer was the plaintive cry of a coyote. Then he began to hear other sounds . . . sounds usually beyond the human senses: He heard the soft footsteps of desert mice scurrying in the brush, the smooth clicking noise of a scorpion preparing to strike, and the slithering of snakes crawling across the warm sand, searching for prey. The snakes seemed to be everywhere.

Frightened, Stephen began to run up a sand dune, but he kept slipping down, unable to reach the top. Then all at once he noticed a reddish glow coming from somewhere behind him, and he turned to see a huge bonfire. Dozens of people appeared, dancing around and leaping across the flames. The people were dressed in flowing robes that looked as if they were made from impossibly delicate folds of snakeskin. The skulls of rattlesnakes, just like the one Sam wore, hung from cords around their necks.

And there was something else, too. In his dream state, Stephen could *sense* an immense shadow of a long, slender body drawn back in a tight S-curve hovering over him. He could feel the steady, hypnotic gaze of its horribly familiar yellowish eyes. It was something dreadful and powerful, something secret, and older than the ancient desert itself. Then, in the flickering firelight, he saw his parents, surrounded by rattlesnakes. The huge shadow moved toward them as the buzzing of the serpents' warning rattles became louder and louder. He knew they were about to strike his parents, but Stephen couldn't move. He tried to scream, but no sound came from his throat. He tried again and—

"YYYEEEEEAAAAAAAA!!" he screamed, sitting straight up in bed.

Liz squealed and fumbled for the light. "What is *wrong* with you!" she yelled. "Are you out of your mind?"

"Mom and Dad! We've got to warn them!" Stephen shrieked, racing for the door.

"Warn them about what?!" Liz yelled. But Stephen didn't stop. Somehow he was sure that his hideous nightmare was going to come true.

When Stephen and Liz got to their parents' room, the door was unlocked. Stephen dashed inside. He couldn't believe it. Their parents' bed was empty! "Mom! Dad!" he screamed again, bolting out of the room to the van just outside. He pounded on the windows, but his parents were nowhere to be found.

"Where are they?" Liz sobbed, growing panicked herself.

"The office!" Stephen gasped. "Maybe they're there!"

The kids ran barefoot across the courtyard. The office was open but deserted.

Liz followed him back outside. "Look!" Stephen pointed. By the eerie glow of the vacancy sign, he could see that the door to bungalow 14 was standing open. Slowly, trying to control his ragged breathing, Stephen walked toward it with Liz on his heels. Somewhere in the back of his frantic mind Stephen registered the fact that the ground was covered with dozens of serpentine tracks leading toward the bungalow. He stopped at the threshold and reached in to snap on the light, but nothing happened.

"Mom? Dad?" Stephen called softly.

"What should we do?" Liz murmured.

Stephen motioned for her to follow him, and the two moved cautiously across the floor into the darkened room.

Stephen abruptly touched something with his foot that made him stop, but in the darkness he couldn't tell what it was. "The drapes," he whispered to Liz. "Open them."

He heard her footsteps and the sound of her fumbling with the drapery cords. Suddenly the drapes swept open and the center of the room was filled with a dull orange light. Stephen's heart pounded rapidly. At his feet he recognized the lifeless body of the old man from bungalow 13. Two others lay nearby in the shadows. He didn't need to look to know they were his parents.

Terrified, Stephen glanced at his sister. She was gaping at the man on the floor, her face frozen in horror. "This isn't real," she moaned. "It's just a terrible nightmare. I'm going to wake up and be home in bed."

"We've got to get out of here!" Stephen cried, lunging toward her.

"I think not," a deep voice hissed from a shrouded corner of the room. Stephen backed closer to his sister as a huge creature slithered into the unearthly light, blocking their escape. Instantly Stephen knew it was the shadowy figure from his dream.

"W-what is it?" Liz stuttered, paralyzed with fear.

The being had the body of an immense rattlesnake, but there was something slightly human about the scaly face, something very familiar about its yellowish eyes.

"Now that you are here," the thing hissed, "I *insissssst* that you stay. I am in command of powers you cannot comprehend. Powers that were already ancient when this desert was still young. But I *need* your life force. My continued survival depends on it."

Stephen took a step to one side, and the creature struck at him, its long fangs bared. It reared back and struck again, missing him by inches. It was toying with him. All at once a dark figure appeared in the open doorway. It was Sam.

"Do something!" Stephen shouted to the man. "Help us!"

"That weak-minded fool cannot help you," the creature whispered viciously. "He will do as he is commanded."

"I told you to leave," Sam answered sadly as he turned away. "You had your chance, but . . ." His voice trailed off as he walked outside, closing and locking the door, forever sealing in the sounds of their screams.

By the time Sam reached the office, the cries had stopped. He leaned wearily against the wall for a moment and looked out at the first signs of the coming dawn. A dusty station wagon turned off the road, rolling to a stop in the motel parking lot. While his family slept, a tired-looking traveler stepped from the vehicle and walked toward the office, the vacancy sign gleaming in the early morning gloom.

The Gift

ebecca slowly spun the globe in her dad's office until it turned to the outline of Southeast Asia. She ran her finger down the Malay Peninsula and stopped at the southern tip.

"Singapore," she said, liking the way it sounded. "Aunt Evelyn sure is lucky to get to go there."

Her father looked up from the computer screen at his desk. "She goes wherever the magazine sends her," he commented. "It's her job."

Rebecca's Aunt Evelyn was a journalist. She wrote about all kinds of faraway places. But best of all, whenever she went somewhere she'd send wonderful souvenirs to Rebecca.

"So what'd you get this time?" her dad asked.

Rebecca looked at the small package in her hand. It was wrapped in brown paper, and there were two rows of foreign postage stamps in the upper right-hand corner.

"I don't know yet," she replied. She'd been savoring the little package ever since the mail carrier had brought it fifteen minutes before. Finally she slipped her finger under an open seam in the paper and ripped it slowly. Inside there was a note and something wrapped in coarse tissue paper. Rebecca pulled away the paper.

"Oh, wow!" she exclaimed. "It's cool!" She held up an ivory-white hair clip. It was carved into a delicate spray of curling leaves and exotic flowers.

"That's lovely," her father said, admiring the gift.

Rebecca opened the note and read quietly for a moment. "It's elephant ivory from Africa," she announced finally. "Aunt Evelyn says it was carved in Hong Kong, and she found it in a little shop in Singapore. She says that you can tell that it's real elephant ivory because it has a tiny, light diamond pattern that you can see on the back." Flipping over the clip, Rebecca examined it closely. "There it is," she said. Walking to the mirror, she held the clip up against her dark hair. "I can't wait to wear it to school on Monday."

• • • • • • • • • •

"You are so lucky," Sandy said with envy when Rebecca showed off her gift to several of her classmates at school. "You're always getting stuff."

"True," Rebecca agreed smugly. "But this is special. It's made out of real elephant ivory which is very hard to get."

"There's a reason for that," Tanya said softly.

"Oh, really?" Rebecca said with a scowl. Tanya was new in school. Sandy had kind of made friends with her, but Rebecca didn't like her and didn't mind showing it. "And what do *you* know about it?"

Tanya looked at the others. She hesitated, searching for the right words. "I've heard that lots of African elephants die because of poaching, and that the sale of ivory has been banned. Your gift is really pretty, but—"

"What's poaching?" Krystal interrupted.

"It's what people call it when the elephants are killed illegally for their ivory tusks," Tanya explained. "The tusks are sold to make all kinds of things."

"Like hair clips?" Sandy asked again, shifting her gaze to Rebecca.

"Don't look at me," Rebecca pouted. "I didn't kill any elephants."

"No, I didn't mean to say that you did anything bad," Tanya said thoughtfully. "But if no one bought things made out of ivory, there wouldn't be any reason to kill elephants for it. I just don't think an animal should have to die so its tusks can be made into jewelry and statues and stuff. Besides, elephants are an endangered species."

"So? I don't see what the big deal is," Rebecca said, laughing, though anger still flared in her eyes. "It's not *my* problem. It's not like I live in Africa or anything. Besides, if the elephant wants this part of its tusk back, it can come and get it. Until then, I'll just wear it myself—probably looks better on me anyway."

The other girls giggled, except for Tanya. "I'm sorry if I upset you, but it isn't funny to joke about things like this," she cautioned seriously.

Rebecca waved her hand. "Relax, Tanya. You're just jealous 'cause you don't have a hair clip like mine."

After school, Rebecca had to stay to make up a math test. It was late afternoon by the time she started to walk home, taking her usual shortcut through Lewis Park. She liked the midsize park. There was one area in particular where the surrounding homes weren't visible. It was sort of a dip in the grassy landscape with a tall hedge on one side and a grove of trees and bushes on the other. When she was little, Rebecca had liked to play there and pretend that she was in a real forest.

Now she walked slowly along the dirt path beside the hedge, humming to herself. She could hear the band practicing at the high school in the distance, and the sound of an occasional car passing on the nearby street. Because it was getting late, the shadows on the ground were already lengthening and the air had taken on the misty quality of twilight. For some reason it seemed to be taking longer than usual to reach the end of the grove.

Then all at once an eerie silence settled among the trees, and Rebecca had the odd sensation that there was no longer anything beyond the hedge. Nervously she picked up her pace a little, then stopped and breathed a sigh of relief. The band had started up again. Or had it?

"That's weird," she muttered, straining to hear the soft,

rhythmic sound of drums. A sudden movement on the other side of the hedge made her jump back in alarm, and all of her senses became keenly alert. "Who's there?" she called out. There was no answer, but something big—very big— seemed to be drawing closer. Rebecca began to run.

When she reached the end of the hedge, she stopped in her tracks. The park was completely empty, and the neighborhood beyond was as it should be. Moms and dads were arriving home from work. Lights were going on in homes as darkness fell. And she could even hear the sound of someone's stereo. Everything seemed perfectly normal. So why did she feel so uneasy?

• • • • • • • • • •

The following Friday was a special day for the entire seventh-grade class. The school had arranged for a field trip to the local zoo to see a pair of rare pandas on loan from China. The event began with a zoo official giving the class a talk about the role zoos play in the community, and then he showed slides of the pandas in their natural habitat. Afterward the class broke into smaller groups. Each group had their own guide to give them a tour of the zoo before stopping at the panda compound. Rebecca and Krystal lagged at the back of their group and had a good time making fun of some of the other kids.

"Look," Rebecca whispered, pointing to a spiky-coated porcupine that was waddling around its compound. "Doesn't the hair on that thing remind you of Linda Mazzeril?"

"Yeah," Krystal agreed, giggling. "And it kind of walks like her, too."

The girls continued to make jokes and snicker as the group moved from compound to compound.

"Look who's hanging out with the elephants," Krystal said, nudging Rebecca.

Rebecca rolled her eyes when she saw that it was Tanya. "Why am I not surprised? Hey, Tanya!" she called out. "Are you having a talk with your animal friends?"

Tanya ignored her, so Rebecca and Krystal strolled over to tease her some more.

A deep concrete channel encircled the elephant compound, preventing the animals from escaping, and a low chain-link fence bordered the channel. Rebecca leaned on the fence and studied the two large elephants within. "Hmmm. They're kind of gross. Let's see what they think of my new gift. I like it so much I was thinking of asking my aunt to get me another one." She turned her head and patted her hair, showing off the ivory clip to one of the elephants. "Hey Jumbo, how do you like it?" she joked cruelly.

All at once the larger of the two elephants turned and trotted rapidly toward the channel, stopping at the far edge. Rebecca's nasty grin faded as she saw how the animal reacted.

"You shouldn't taunt them," Tanya warned gently. "You never know what can happen."

That night Rebecca couldn't get the incident out of her mind. It had left her feeling troubled. "I don't see why Tanya has to make such a big deal about elephants," she grumbled aloud as she stood in front of her bedroom mirror. She reached up and brushed her fingers over the carved ivory clip in her hair. The image in the mirror flickered slightly, then the room behind her grew hazy.

"What in the world . . . ?" Rebecca murmured. Her heart began to pound so hard that she could hear its rhythmic pulse. From somewhere behind her, the sound of distant drums matched the rhythm beat for beat. As she stared wide-eyed, Rebecca saw the reflection in the mirror change. Whirling around she found that she was no longer in her room but on an open, grassy plain that stretched as far as she could see. Here and there, scraggly acacia trees stood out starkly against the horizon.

"This is impossible," she gasped. "I'm dreaming!" She took a step and felt her foot sink into something cool and slick. Looking down, she saw that she was standing at the edge of a pool of muddy water. The banks of the pool were crisscrossed by tracks . . . animal tracks of all kinds. It was a huge watering hole, and at the far end, a pair of acacias provided meager shelter from the burning sun. In the oasis of shade stood a small group of African elephants. There were several babies and four or five adults. The largest of them turned in her direction, causing Rebecca to cry out in fear.

"Rebecca! What is going on in here! Are you hurt? What's wrong?"

Suddenly Rebecca felt her father's hands on her shoulders.

"Dad?" she moaned, gazing up at him through tears. "I just . . . I thought that . . . " But looking at his face she knew it was impossible to explain what she had just experienced. "I—I just had a terrible dream!"

"Do you want to tell me about it?" he asked with concern.

She shook her head. "No," she mumbled, beginning to feel foolish. Of course it was only a dream. She had been letting Tanya and all of her mumbo jumbo get to her. "I—I'm just tired from the field trip. I'll be all right."

After her dad left the room, Rebecca slowly removed the ivory clip from her hair, vowing to ignore Tanya from now on. In fact, her fear had now turned to resentment. *She doesn't have any right to tell me what to do*, Rebecca thought angrily. *I'll wear whatever I want to.*

The following day, Tanya had stayed home with a cold, and Rebecca forgot all about what had happened until she walked home alone that afternoon. Taking her usual route through Lewis Park, she hesitated beside the hedge.

"This is ridiculous," she said, scolding herself. "I'm in a public park in broad daylight." Squaring her shoulders, she proceeded along the dirt path. Soon her view of the neighborhood was obscured by trees and bushes. She heaved a relaxed sigh as she rounded the far end of the hedge, but her relief was short-lived.

There, directly ahead of her, stretched the sun-drenched plain she had seen in her mirror the night before. Rebecca could even hear insects buzzing lazily in the tall, dry grass, and she could feel the blazing sun on her hair and face . . . though it had been a cold, cloudy day just moments before. Quickly looking over her shoulder, she saw a pair of acacia trees beside a muddy pond of water. A small family of elephants stood silently watching. The lead animal took several steps toward her.

"I know this isn't happening," Rebecca reassured herself. "I'm imagining this, and my imagination *can't* hurt me." But when the phantom beast began to charge, Rebecca screamed and ran.

As her feet pounded against the burning ground, she frantically searched for any avenue of escape. All at once she saw what appeared to be a deep, narrow gully and raced toward it as the maddened animal quickly closed the gap between them. Feeling as if her lungs would burst, Rebecca made one final effort and leapt outward toward the gully. Suddenly the creature stopped and trumpeted in victory, as the vista of the African plains began to fade and her own neighborhood swam into focus. It was the last thing Rebecca ever saw. She never even felt the blow as something hit her hard from the side, tossing her into the air like a rag doll.

"She just ran out into the street right in front of me!" a frantic truck driver groaned to a police officer who was jotting notes in a small pad. "I—I didn't have time to react."

"That's right," an older woman chimed in. "That little girl came flying around that hedge like she was being chased by something. I saw the whole thing."

A few feet away two other officers stood at the curb. "She probably didn't even know what hit her," the first man said sadly. He knelt and picked up a small, sharp, ivory-colored object from the sidewalk. It looked like the broken tip of a tusk.

"Something must have really scared her," his partner reflected. "I wonder what it was?"

"We'll probably never know," the first officer answered, tossing the object into the gutter, where it rolled to a stop beside a broken ivory hair clip.

Adrift

Lucas picked up a dry, twisted length of mesquite and threw it on the fire. Almost immediately, flames swirled around it, causing the wood to crackle. Glowing sparks floated up into the warm night air and were soon lost against the backdrop of the star-studded sky.

For a while everyone sat in silence around the wide fire pit they had dug in the desert sand. Lucas was thrilled that his parents had allowed him to go on this spring weekend camping trip with three of his friends. Of course, if Andrew's older brother, Dennis, hadn't offered to come along as a chaperone, Lucas's mom and dad probably wouldn't have agreed to it.

Dennis Kwan was studying at the local university to be a botanist, and he had made dozens of field trips into the plains and foothills of the southern Mojave Desert to study plants. He knew the area very well, and was literally a stockpile of neat facts and stories about the desert.

"Did you know that the creosote bush may be the oldest living thing on earth?" Dennis asked. He held up a branch for the boys to see. It was covered with tiny green leaves and tipped with little flowers the color of butter.

"No way," Andrew said with a mischievous smile. "Ms. Norman is the oldest living thing on earth."

Everyone laughed. Ms. Norman was the bus driver who drove most of them daily to and from Desert Vale Middle School.

Ted's face grew serious. "So how old *is* that stuff?" he asked, pointing to the branch in Dennis's hand.

"Some of it is as much as nine thousand years old," the twenty-year-old stated.

"What do you mean by 'some of it'?" Rick questioned.

Dennis smiled, glad to see the boys were interested in the subject he loved. "The way it works is that the creosote starts with one plant, then produces a ring of new plants around it. Those produce new ones and so on, in some cases for thousands of years. So you see, they're all really just clones of the first plant. That's why you can say that a ring of creosote is as old as the original plant."

Ted stared in awe at the ring of scraggly plants that grew near the campsite. "Is all that creosote?"

Dennis nodded. "There are lots of strange and unusual

things out here," he added in a mystical voice. He raised his eyebrow. "You might find some of them quite surprising."

"Like what?" Andrew asked, knowing his brother also had a talent for telling great spooky stories around a campfire.

"I don't know if I should tell you." Dennis pretended to be hesitant. "You might not sleep too well if I do."

"Come on," Lucas begged.

The others joined in, and Dennis finally agreed to tell them a story. He leaned toward the fire. The flames caused ribbons of light and shadow to flicker across his face, as he began.

"This is a tale of an amazing ghost ship," he whispered dramatically. "A Spanish galleon has sailed in search of its lost treasure for nearly three hundred years."

"Wait a minute," Kevin said with a look of disbelief. "We're in the Mojave Desert. The last time I checked, there weren't many ships sailing through here."

Ted, Rick, and Lucas burst into laughter.

"Go ahead and laugh, ye of little faith," Dennis snarled in mock indignation. "It just so happens that a long time ago, when Mexico was known as New Spain, Spanish ships sailed in the Gulf of California. Sometimes those ships carried treasures meant to be transported back to Spain." He paused and looked at each of the four boys in turn. "One in particular carried a fortune in pearls, but that ill-fated ship never reached its destination."

"What happened to it?" Lucas asked.

Dennis leaned back. "That was the year of the great floods," he answered, as if telling the tale from his own experience. "The Colorado River overflowed and the unfortunate ship sailed much farther north than it should have. Eventually it became grounded somewhere in this area. Then when the flood waters receded, the ship was stranded in the desert. Most of the crew wanted to set out on foot, but the captain and a few loyal sailors refused to leave the treasure that they had vowed to protect."

"So what did they do?" Andrew murmured. He thought he'd heard all of his brother's stories, but this one was new to him.

Dennis looked right into his brother's eyes. "The crew murdered the captain and all of his followers," he responded with contempt. "Then they buried the treasure somewhere in the foothills. I expect they thought they might be rescued, and then they could come back for it. But with the exception of one lone survivor, who was discovered near death somewhere around here, none of the sailors were ever seen again . . . not *alive*, that is."

"Here it comes," Rick whispered to Lucas. Both boys rolled their eyes and waited for the scary finish.

"To this day," Dennis continued, "a ghostly ship and crew are occasionally sighted sailing the desert in search of the lost treasure . . . the murderous crew spurred on by their phantom captain." He put his finger to his lips, then looked from side to side, peering into the shadows beyond the glow of the fire. "Some say that if you try hard enough, you can hear the creak of the rigging and the fluttering of the sails in the wind."

Everyone sat quietly for a moment. "So," Kevin asked at last, "does that mean the treasure is still out here?"

"That's what they say," Dennis answered, shifting into a

94

more matter-of-fact tone. "I've even seen prospectors in this area looking for it. But if a chest full of pearls is really buried in these foothills, finding it will take a lot of luck."

"Didn't the survivor tell anyone where it was buried?" Lucas asked.

Dennis shook his head. "It wouldn't have done any good if he had. Sandstorms can whip up out here without any warning, and once they've passed, things look different. Some landmarks can be covered up, and others uncovered. It's easy to see how something could be hopelessly lost."

"There may be a treasure out here," Rick said, rubbing his stomach, "but right now I'd settle for a hot dog."

Everyone agreed, and soon they were all roasting juicy frankfurters over the fire.

Shortly afterward the boys wriggled into their sleeping bags that were rolled out on the dry ground.

"Hey, Andrew," Lucas whispered. "You still awake?"

"Yeah," his friend replied quietly.

"I've been thinking. It would really be cool to find that treasure. Maybe we could look for it."

There was no answer.

"Andrew?" Lucas tried again.

"Shhhhh." Andrew moved a little closer and spoke softly so he was certain that only Lucas could hear him. "I just got an excellent idea," he said with a devilish tone. "It'll be a great gag, but I don't want to talk about it now. I'll tell you in the morning."

"Cool," said Lucas.

Andrew had a reputation for playing pranks, and Lucas was glad he was going to be in on it instead of being the brunt of it. Rolling over onto his back, he put his hands behind his head and gazed up at the stars, wondering what trick his friend had in mind.

• • • • • • • • • •

The next morning, by the time the sun was up, Dennis had started a fire in the sand pit. While the boys rolled up their sleeping bags, he started scrambling eggs in a large iron skillet.

After breakfast the boys spent the day exploring a gorge about half a mile from their campsite. To get to it they had to hike across a wide, sandy plain with their day packs. Here and there among the waves of sand dunes they found lavender patches of tiny flowers that Dennis identified as sand verbena.

Lucas had all but forgotten about Andrew's prank, and then once they were in the gorge the mischievous boy pulled him aside and pointed to a canyon a few hundred yards farther north.

"There's an abandoned mine in that canyon," Andrew whispered. "It's loaded with old boards and empty crates left behind by the miners. Dennis has taken me up there a few times." He grinned. "It'll be perfect."

"Perfect for what?" Lucas asked in confusion.

Andrew's grin grew wider and his eyes sparkled. "All we have to do is sneak up there tonight and get a crate that's still in pretty good shape. We can fill it full of sand and rocks to weight it down, then we half-bury it near the campsite where one of the guys will find it in the morning." He tried to contain his laughter. "I guarantee whoever finds it will be convinced he's discovered the lost treasure. Then everyone will go crazy trying to dig for it."

Lucas frowned. "Nobody's going to fall for that."

"Oh, come on," Andrew pleaded. "It's worth a try. If it works, it'll be a lot of laughs."

Lucas shrugged. "I guess," he said, unconvinced.

Later that evening, once everyone was asleep, Andrew and Lucas crept silently from the campsite.

"You sure you know where you're going?" Lucas questioned once they were far enough away not to be heard.

Andrew grinned at him. "No sweat. I've been up here a bunch of times. Besides," he gestured toward the sky. "This full moon is so bright that we'll be able to see the campsite even from a distance. There's no way we can get lost."

Lucas looked at the sky. Andrew did have a point. The night was crystal clear.

"OK," he said to his friend. "You're the boss."

A light, warm wind had started to blow as the boys began to cross the dunes. Lucas's feet sank deep into the sand with each step, making it difficult to walk. By the time they reached the canyon he was exhausted. To make things worse, the wind had picked up. It moaned eerily through the pass, lifting clouds of sand into the air and making it hard to see.

"I don't like this," Lucas said nervously. "Maybe we should go back."

"It isn't much farther," Andrew coaxed. "We're already here, so we might as well get what we came for."

"Yeah, but—" Lucas slipped as he climbed over a low,

rocky outcropping and fell to the ground with a grunt. "Ow!" he yelped, grabbing his hand as a few drops of blood trickled out from a jagged cut on his thumb.

"Bummer," Andrew said, flopping down beside him. "What did you cut it on?"

Lucas scanned the immediate area and noticed an inch-wide band of metal protruding from the coarse sand under the outcropping. "Probably on that," he answered, pointing to the metal band a couple of feet behind him.

Andrew crawled over and scooped away some of the loose sand around the metal. "It's attached to something. Help me with this."

With his uninjured hand, Lucas helped his friend dig. In moments the boys uncovered what appeared to be the rotting top of a fairly large chest. The metal strip was one of two bands that had been wrapped around the chest to seal it shut. Unlike the first band, the other one was still intact, but badly corroded. Andrew pulled out his Swiss army knife and pried at it until it popped open.

The two boys looked at each other for a moment, each knowing what the other was thinking. Finally Andrew placed his hands on the lid of the chest and slowly lifted it open. Then he gasped in wonder. Lucas couldn't even gasp. All he could do was stare, speechless. Inside, dozens—perhaps hundreds—of huge pearls glimmered in the moonlight.

"I don't believe this," Andrew stood up and shouted into the rising wind. "It's real! The treasure is real, and *we* discovered it!"

All at once Lucas found his voice. "Let's try to get it out!"

Together the boys struggled to lift the chest out from

under the low rocky shelf, but it wouldn't budge. "We have to get some help!" Lucas yelled, trying to shield his face from the blowing sand. He and Andrew scrambled to their feet and started to head for the mouth of the canyon. "Wait!" Lucas shouted over the howling wind. He ran back to the ancient chest and grabbed a large pearl. "Let's go," he said. "Now I've got proof so the others will believe us."

Once they reached the end of the canyon, it was clear that they could go no farther. The plain between them and the campsite was a mass of shifting sand that stung their faces and hands, and it was getting worse by the minute— *much* worse.

"We won't get far in this," Lucas hollered. "We'll have to find some shelter and wait it out!"

Andrew nodded, and together they squeezed into a wide cleft between two immense boulders. The wind screeched and wailed like a wounded animal. Lucas pressed his eyes shut and covered his ears. Finally the terrible blast began to subside and the sandstorm was over as quickly as it had started.

"Let's get back," Andrew urged, and Lucas didn't need to be told twice. He wriggled from his hiding place and followed his friend to the mouth of the canyon. Everything was strangely silent. The moon had slipped behind a thick band of clouds, and there was an unearthly chill in the air.

"I don't like this," Lucas muttered. "It doesn't feel right."

"Hush!" Andrew ordered, straining to see into the darkness ahead of them. "Did you here that?"

Lucas listened. There *was* something, but what he thought it was just couldn't be. But as the sound grew louder and closer, he couldn't deny that it was a creaking

noise, like timbers rubbing against each other. Peering into the night, the boys caught sight of something moving somehow *above* the sand dunes. *Run!* Lucas's mind screamed. But no matter how much he willed his trembling body to move, Lucas could not budge. He felt as if his fear had turned him to stone. He sensed that Andrew, too, shared his terror.

There above the darkened plain, a pale, glowing ghost ship rose and fell on the invisible waves of a spectral sea. The ship's sails billowed out as if a brisk wind filled them. As the boys gaped helplessly, the ship sailed closer . . . close enough so that Lucas could make out shadowy figures on deck. It glided within a few yards of them and then stopped, blocking off any hope of escape. The air became dense and reeked of salt and seawater.

Finding it hard to breathe, Lucas felt as if he were drowning. He struggled to move, to save himself, but everything became hazy. When his vision cleared, he found himself lying next to Andrew on the rotting deck of an ancient ship.

"W-where are we?" Andrew stammered.

Lucas said nothing, fearing the only possible answer. The smell of dampness and mold filled his nostrils, and he was chilled to the bone.

"Noooooooo!" Lucas wailed in terror as phantom hands gripped him and shoved him below deck and into a small chamber. He landed in a heap on the floor, and beside him was Andrew.

Something walked slowly and carefully across the wooden floorboards, then stopped a few inches from where the boys huddled. Lucas risked a glance upward and tried not to gag. The spirit of the ship's captain leaned over them, the grisly head wound that had caused his death still oozing on his ghostly forehead. When he opened his mouth to speak, a gust of foul air reeking of death and decay made the boys recoil in disgust.

"Where did you find this?" the gruesome creature asked in a hollow voice. Lucas saw that it held the pearl he had taken from the chest.

"I—I can show you," he stuttered, forcing himself to speak. "If you let us go."

"Done!" the hideous specter agreed.

Within moments, Lucas and Andrew were leaning over the railing of the ghost ship as it sailed silently along the canyon wall.

"I don't see it!" Andrew sobbed. "I can't see the spot where we found the treasure."

Lucas scanned every inch of the canyon, but the low outcropping of rock was nowhere to be found. During the powerful storm, the sands of the canyon floor had shifted completely, and nothing was familiar. All of the heaps and piles of sand and rock looked the same. There was no way he could pick out the spot where the chest lay buried.

"It was here!" he cried, but already the ship was turning back toward the murky, phantom sea that it was doomed to sail until the elusive treasure was finally found.

"Now you must join our search," bellowed the spirit captain. "Even if it lasts forever!"

The Final Draft

anessa's mother looked around happily. "It's a perfect house!" she exclaimed. "Can't you just imagine a murder taking place here?"

Vanessa nodded and pushed aside the wispy white drapes at the large bay window in the living room. Outside, a wide expanse of closely clipped green lawn swept to the top of a low cliff overlooking the Atlantic Ocean. Vanessa's twin sister, Samantha, was already walking along the edge of the bluff in the early morning sunlight, trying to find the quickest path to the beach below. "Is somebody going to get shoved off the cliff?" Vanessa asked innocently.

"Nope," her dad answered as he stepped through the open front door carrying two overstuffed suitcases. "I think that's too obvious. We need something more . . . sinister, more . . ."

"Gothic?" her mom offered.

Vanessa smiled. Having a pair of screenwriters for parents was never dull. Once when her mom and dad were asked to write a script about voodoo, the girls got to go along for a week on a Caribbean island. Another time their parents had taken them to see the ruins of the Egyptian pyramids for background on a tale about an ancient mummy. Now Vanessa's mom and dad had gotten an offer to come up with a new script for a scary murder mystery, so they'd simply rented the spookiest home they could find on the coast of Maine and packed up the family for the whole summer. Here they were, ready to work on an idea.

"This place is great!" Samantha exclaimed, letting the screen door slam behind her as she raced inside. "The backyard is huge and there's an old-fashioned swing, flower gardens, fruit trees, and even a birdhouse. Come on, Vanessa," she urged. "Come check it out with me."

"Not yet, young ladies," their mom said, halting the girls at the door and pointing to their suitcases. "These need to be unpacked first. You'll have plenty of time to explore later."

By the time their mom called them downstairs for a lunch of deli sandwiches and potato salad, Vanessa and Samantha had put all of their things away in the room they were to share. It was a marvelous, old-fashioned room, with delicate rosebud wallpaper and a window seat with plump pink seat cushions. Their parents had set up the den as an office and had already spent a couple of hours working.

Once the girls sat down at the table for lunch, their parents told them a little about the story.

"The main point is that the ghost of the murdered woman is trying to come back in order to identify the person who killed her to the people who are now living in the house she was killed in ten years ago. They, of course, have no idea that the murder had ever taken place," Vanessa's mom explained as the girls spooned potato salad onto their plates.

"Cool," said Samantha. "I like it."

"Yeah, Mom," Vanessa agreed. "What happens next?"

Their mother leaned over the table as if about to share a secret with them. "The spirit leads one of the main characters—probably the daughter—to the murder weapon that has been hidden in the house all that time."

Vanessa's dad helped himself to some potato chips from a large bowl on the table. "More important, the phantom will then lead somebody to her very own corpse," he added, a twinkle in his eye. "The police think that the dead woman jumped off a cliff and her body was washed out to sea," he said dramatically. "What they *don't* know is that she was really murdered by her cousin, who hid the body in the old well."

"That's a great idea, Dad," Vanessa said. "Did you guys think up the whole plot this morning?"

Her mother smiled. "Well, we haven't exactly worked the whole plot out yet, but, yes, most of the idea just seemed to flow onto the computer."

"It's this old house," Vanessa's dad declared as he toyed with his turkey on rye. "I feel almost like it's focusing our creative energies . . . magnifying them."

Samantha rolled her eyes at Vanessa as if to say *Oh brother . . . writers!*

"What made you think of using a well to hide the body?" Vanessa asked, trying not to laugh at her sister's antics.

"There's an old well near the laurel hedge," their mother answered. "It gave us the idea."

"I didn't see a well," Samantha commented, raising her eyebrows. "And I walked all the way around that hedge this morning."

"It's there," her dad said, finishing the last bite of his sandwich. "So, what do you think about taking some time off this weekend and having a picnic on the beach?"

Everyone agreed that it was a great idea, and for the moment the subject of the well—and the script—was forgotten.

After lunch the girls went outside together and walked the length of the overgrown laurel hedge, first up one side, then down the other.

"This must be it," Vanessa guessed, pointing to an ancient-looking gray stone well that was half hidden within a tangle of tall grass and wild rosebushes. A wooden crossbeam had a corroded bucket hanging from it by a rotting rope connected to a metal crank. Vanessa gave the crank handle a tug. "It's rusted solid," she said, disappointed.

Samantha furrowed her brow. "That well was *not* here this morning. I would have *seen* it."

"Oh, come on, Sam," Vanessa said, laughing. "It didn't suddenly appear out of nowhere. You just didn't notice it with all this stuff growing around it." She paused, then gnarled her fingers like a witch. In a spooky voice she added,

"If this is a ghost well, then maybe there really is a body down there." Vanessa pulled away several overhanging vines and exposed a wooden lid that sealed the well shut.

"I would have *seen* it," Samantha muttered. "I *know* I would have."

"Come on," urged Vanessa, ignoring her. "Let's see if we can get this lid off."

• • • • • • • • • • •

When they went to bed that night Vanessa was still too excited about being in the creepy old house to sleep. She listened to her sister's calm, relaxed breathing, which was almost in perfect time with the soothing rhythm of the ocean waves rolling onto the nearby beach. Through the open window she could even hear crickets chirping. Vanessa listened more closely.

Those aren't crickets, she thought, slipping out of bed. *It must be the swing squeaking.* She went to the window and looked at the swing, but it was hanging perfectly still from a sturdy branch of the huge oak tree in the center of the yard. The lawn was bathed in moonlight, and the edge of the cliff stood out clearly against the blackness of the ocean beyond. Vanessa turned her head to one side, trying to focus on the odd noise. It was coming from the darkness along the laurel hedge.

"What are you doing?" Samantha asked, startling her sister.

"I heard something," Vanessa whispered. "Come here and listen."

Samantha joined her sister at the window. "It sounds like somebody's twisting a big piece of metal," she guessed.

Vanessa's eyes opened wide. "The well!" she gasped. "Maybe somebody's turning the crank!"

Samantha and Vanessa looked at each other, then turned their gaze back to the hedge.

"There!" Samantha exclaimed, pointing out into the gloomy yard. "What's that moving down there?"

Vanessa squinted. She could barely make out the dark shadow at the far end of the hedge. It was inching slowly toward the house. All at once she heard a sound on the stairs and grabbed Samantha's arm. It was coming closer, the polished wooden steps creaking under its weight as it mounted them one by one.

"Don't forget to check the front door," their mom called quietly to their dad.

Both girls sighed with relief. A moment later they heard their father also climbing the stairs. The hall light snapped off, and the door to the master bedroom closed.

Vanessa's heartbeat slowly returned to normal. "They must be turning in for the night," she whispered as she peered down once again at the backyard. There was nothing out of the ordinary. "Do you think we should tell them what we saw?"

"What *did* we see?" Samantha asked. "We're just letting this place get to us. I mean, after hearing Mom and Dad's story about the well and all . . . maybe we were just—"

"Imagining things," Vanessa said with a giggle. "Mom and Dad would be proud. Maybe we'll be writers too." She cast a final glance outside and, reassured that everything was as it should be, returned to bed.

The following day they explored the shoreline of the beautiful sandy cove at the bottom of the cliff. Vanessa even braved the chilly Atlantic to take a brisk swim. Samantha rolled up the legs of her jeans and did some beachcombing, filling a plastic bucket with shells, rocks, and odd pieces of driftwood. At lunchtime their parents took a break, and the family had a picnic lunch on the beach. Both Samantha and Vanessa had fallen in love with the area.

"I can't imagine ever wanting to leave this incredible place!" Vanessa exclaimed.

Exhausted from all of the sun and exercise, the twins went to bed early. Vanessa snuggled under the covers and drifted off to sleep immediately. She awoke to the pressure of Samantha's hand clasped tightly on her wrist.

"What?" Vanessa started to ask drowsily. Samantha pressed her finger to her sister's lips to stop her from speaking. Samantha's face was white with fear, and Vanessa instantly realized why—they were not alone in the room! Terrified, she drew in a lungful of foul, dank air that smelled of mildew. *What's going on?* her mind screamed as the tiny hairs on the back of her neck stood on end. Now painfully alert to every sound, Vanessa heard someone feeling along the molding that framed the window, and what she saw chilled her blood. Something that resembled a woman was leaning over the window seat, but it *wasn't* a woman. It was dark like a shadow, but had a faint glimmer to it as if it were wet, giving it a sheen like that of polished marble. Whatever it was, it seemed to be searching for something.

Vanessa drew the covers back over her head as slowly as she could. Samantha, now under the covers with her, was trembling with fright, gripping Vanessa's hand so tightly that she was cutting off the circulation in her fingers. Desperately trying to control her own ragged breathing, Vanessa was beginning to think that her fear would stop her from taking another breath at all. Suddenly the mildewy air turned fresh and smelled of grass and jasmine. Cautiously risking a peek out from under the covers, she cast a furtive glance at the window . . . but there was nothing there.

Heaving a sigh of relief, Vanessa sat up and turned on the light beside the bed. Samantha sat up too. Her face was pale and her eyes were red, as though she had been squeezing them tightly shut.

"Were we just dreaming?" Vanessa murmured hopefully.

"I—I don't think so," Samantha answered, her voice faltering, and then her eyes widened. "Look!" she cried.

Vanessa followed her sister's horrified gaze to the hardwood floor. A line of small, damp footprints led from the door to the window.

"I'm getting Mom and Dad!" Vanessa shrieked, tossing aside the covers. She raced down the stairs with Samantha close behind.

They found their parents were still hard at work in the den. Their dad was pacing back and forth, reading through pages of printed notes, while their mother pecked at the keyboard of the computer.

"Dad! Mom!" Vanessa shouted. "There was someone . . . some*thing* in our room!

"Yeah," Samantha gasped. "It was like a dark shadow, and it—"

"Wait a minute. Slow down," their father said calmly

holding up his hand. "The two of you must have been dreaming. I'm sure there's nothing in your room." He dropped his notes on the table and wrapped his arms around his terrified daughters. "Come on. Let's all go up and see, shall we?"

"I don't want to," Samantha protested, breaking away and going to stand next to their mother.

Slipping off his glasses, their dad rubbed his eyes. "Just what was it again you thought you saw?"

"It was a woman, but more like a shadow," Vanessa said with a shiver. "It was dark but it kind of glowed . . ."

Samantha nodded absentmindedly, for her eyes had drifted to the script her parents were writing on the computer. She stared at the screen and mumbled, "It was dark like a shadow, but had a faint glimmer to it as if it were wet, giving it a sheen like that of polished marble. Whatever it was, it seemed to be searching for something."

"She's right. That's exactly—" Vanessa paused when she realized that her sister was reading from the screen.

"The thing keeps up its search," Samantha read on. "Horrified, the young girl slowly draws the covers back over her head." She stopped and slowly looked up at Vanessa. "It's all right here in the script," she said stiffly. "Even the part about the footprints."

"I don't understand," Vanessa said, looking from her father to her mother. "What you wrote—it came true. It really happened."

"Yes," Samantha said. "It happened . . . to *us*!"

Her father shook his head. "Maybe we're all just getting caught up in this thing," he said calmly. "You two probably just overheard your mother and I talking about the story, and without even realizing it, you had a dream about the exact same thing."

"Of course. Your father's right," their mother agreed. "There are so many kinks in this plot, and we've been working so hard to get them ironed out. Somehow it all must be having an effect on you girls. That's the only possible explanation."

"No," Vanessa said softly, looking toward the stairs that led to their room. "It *isn't* the only explanation. I think this place really *is* haunted."

After their dad had looked into every closet and corner, the girls agreed to go back to bed. Still, they insisted on leaving the light on.

The sun was just a glowing semicircle over the deep blue of the Atlantic when Samantha shook Vanessa awake. "Come on," she urged. "I want to go down to the well and see if the cover is still on."

Vanessa rubbed her eyes. "Why?" she asked.

"Come *on*," Samantha insisted, tossing Vanessa's jeans onto the bed. "Think about it. How else would you explain those damp footprints?"

Within a few minutes the girls were rounding the end of the laurel hedge. Vanessa froze in her tracks. "This isn't possible," she said in disbelief. Samantha gaped wordlessly. Where the decrepit well should have been, draped in a chaotic web of grass and wild roses, there now stood a pristine white gazebo. It was surrounded by a dainty half-circle of well-tended rosebushes.

"What is happening here?" Vanessa moaned. She

grabbed Samantha's hand and together they ran around the hedge and across the lawn. Gasping for breath, they both clambered onto the porch and, throwing open the screen door, charged into the house.

"Mom! Dad!" Vanessa screamed.

"We're in here," her father called, appearing in the doorway to the den. "What's wrong?"

"It's the well," Samantha sputtered. "We went to see if there would be anything different about it after what happened last night, but it's completely gone! There's a gazebo there instead, and all the bushes have been trimmed, and—"

She stopped. Both of her parents were looking at her quizzically.

"What are you talking about?" her mother finally asked in a mystified tone. "There's no well around here."

"But there was," Vanessa answered uncertainly. "It was right behind the laurel hedge."

Her father shook his head and grinned. "You would think that *you* two were the ones who stayed up working all night instead of *us*." He took a gulp of coffee from his ceramic mug. "There's no well back there. We just wrote about one."

"Your dad's right. We just made up the well," her mother said, the corners of her mouth turning up in a pleasant smile. "We just used our imagination, and I'll bet that's what you two are doing too . . . unless you're trying to play a joke on us."

Confused, Vanessa glanced at a bewildered-looking Samantha.

"Well, none of this matters anyway," their father said

laughing. "The idea wasn't coming together, so we dumped it."

"Dumped it?" Vanessa asked.

"Yup. We erased the file a couple of hours ago and started work on a new idea," he explained enthusiastically. "It's much more exciting. It's about this—"

Just then the telephone rang. "I'll tell you about it in a little bit," their dad said, as he reached for the receiver and flopped onto the couch.

Vanessa felt a wave of relief. No matter how hard her parents tried to explain away the strange things they'd seen, she was certain that the weird occurrences had something to do with the script they were writing. True, maybe she and Samantha just dreamed everything. But *maybe* their father had been right when he said that there was something about the old house that focused their creative energies, making the events they wrote about real. In any case, it no longer mattered. The script was gone, and so was the well, along with whatever lurked in its moldy depths.

"Why don't we go and fix a nice hot breakfast?" She heard her mother saying. Vanessa turned to follow Samantha toward the kitchen, when she caught a few words of her dad's telephone conversation.

"You'll love it!" he was saying enthusiastically to someone on the other end of the line. "We stayed up all night to finish the first scene. It starts with this family that rents a house on the coast of New England. It's a tranquil spot and the house is a great old place. You know the type . . . old-fashioned swing in the backyard . . . beautiful white gazebo surrounded by rosebushes. Anyway . . . "

Vanessa stood riveted to the spot. *That's where the gazebo came from,* she thought with a growing sense of dread.

". . . the family is totally unaware that this huge asteroid is hurtling through space on a collision course with Earth. We're talking an asteroid the size of Mount Everest."

"No!" Vanessa screamed aloud at her father. "Don't you see. What you write in this house comes true!"

Her father looked at her sternly and held up his hand to quiet her as he continued his conversation, "So get this—it's all done in flashbacks. It begins when the asteroid hits. It splashes down somewhere in the Atlantic Ocean just off the coast of New England, and—"

"Noooooo!!" Vanessa howled as the ground began to tremble, then rock fiercely. "You've got to erase the script!"

But her warning was too late. The last thing Vanessa saw was the sky blazing from bright blue to fiery, brilliant white. Then the house shivered and swayed and finally burst into splinters of wood and showers of glass in the earth-shattering explosion that inevitably followed as an immense asteroid plunged into the Atlantic Ocean only a mile away.

The Exchange

J avier's mother stood at the door to his room. Her forehead wrinkled into a frown. "I thought you said you were doing homework," she complained wearily. "You told me you didn't have time to help with the dishes because you had a book report due tomorrow."

Stretched out on his bed, Javier looked at her over the cover of a comic book. "I got tired of working on it," he said simply and returned his gaze to the comic book. It was his favorite character, the Savage Sorcerer, a dark sort of medieval supernatural being who had mastered the art of magic and used it to get what he wanted.

His mother sighed. "I give up. I'm tired of always having

to nag to get you to do anything. We'll just wait until your father gets home and see what he has to say." She closed the door and left him alone.

Javier let out a short, humorless laugh. His father worked the swing shift and rarely even saw his family except on weekends, so he wasn't worried about his mother's threat. He went back to studying his comic book. There was an illustration of a tall, muscular man dressed in black with a hooded cape, and he was blasting an enemy with magical flashes of energy that shot from his eyes.

If I had powers like that, I'd never have to worry about homework or chores or anything, Javier thought enviously. *I could do whatever I wanted.* He glanced up at the collection of books and magic kits that he had constantly wasted his allowance on.

"They're no use," he muttered. "If I'm ever going to have *real* magical powers, I'd have to learn from a real sorcerer."

Tossing the book to the floor, he walked to the window and stared up at the crescent moon. "I'd give anything for powers like that," he whispered. "Anything."

• • • • • • • • • • •

On weekends Javier's mother usually took him and his grandmother shopping, first at the local mall and then at the grocery store. His grandmother didn't drive. In fact, she was a little afraid of cars; Javier figured it was because she was so old. He didn't like being around old people. He thought they were too slow and always talked about things that happened a long time ago as if those things were actually still important. Today, as usual, he was impatient with his grandmother, and as soon as they got to the mall, he made an excuse to go off on his own.

"Meet us at the pharmacy in one hour," his mother called after him as Javier headed for the escalators.

"Yeah, yeah," he muttered, stepping onto the first moving step. There was a video arcade on the second floor, *and* a small magic shop. The shop had all the usual stuff, but it was better than nothing.

After a few minutes in the video arcade, Javier strolled to the magic shop and halted in surprise. Instead of being filled with a jumble of merchandise on display, the front window was covered by a black curtain. In the lower right corner was a sign that read UNDER NEW MANAGEMENT and below that ERRAND PERSON WANTED, APPLY WITHIN.

Curious, Javier stepped inside. Gloomy and dim, the shop was filled with the smell of incense and scented candles. A tape was playing that sounded like people chanting, but he couldn't figure out where the sound was coming from. Slowly he explored the shop. In one glass showcase there were trays of glittering crystals, pots of what looked like multicolored sand, tiny packets of dried herbs, and small sculptures of mythical creatures such as dragons and gargoyles.

The other case held typical magic tricks, as well as cards for fortune-telling and scrolls of astrological signs. Well-stocked bookcases lined the room, and on the wall, behind the old-fashioned brass cash register, hung an aging publicity poster of a handsome young man dressed in the style of the 1940s. Javier read the claim below aloud: "Reynaldo, the World's Greatest Magician."

119

"And so I was," a voice declared dramatically.

Startled, Javier jumped, then whirled around to see an elderly man with a halo of snow-white hair who bore a striking resemblance to the dapper fellow in the poster. "I am Reynaldo," the man said. "Are you here about the job? If you are, you need to know that this is no ordinary magic shop with marked cards and boxes with false compartments," he muttered with obvious distaste. "I'm concerned with true magic, not parlor tricks." He scowled. "Now, does the job interest you?"

Javier had been just snooping around, but what the man said gave him an idea. Maybe this was the chance he was looking for to learn something about real magic . . . even if the guy *did* seem like a grouch. "Yes," Javier declared with a forced smile. "I'd like to apply for the job."

Reynaldo raised an eyebrow and stroked his chin with the long, slender fingers of one gloved hand. "I require someone to run errands and do odd jobs Saturdays and Sundays," he said. "So if you want to spend your weekends with your family or catching up on homework . . . "

"Oh, that's not important," Javier interrupted.

Reynaldo eyed Javier up and down for a moment. "You're rather young," he said finally. "What about friends? Don't you want to spend time with them on the weekends?"

Javier shook his head. "Nah, I don't like other kids very much. I can't wait until I grow up."

After staring at Javier for another moment, the old man reached behind the counter and pulled out a crisp sheet of paper and a pen. "Fill out this form," he instructed curtly. "I'll let you know."

When Javier got a call from the magic shop a week later, he was thrilled. He reported to work early Saturday morning, planning to learn everything that he could from the old magician.

Finding the front door was unlocked, he wasn't sure what to do. He entered and saw several candles already flickering in their holders. The place appeared to be deserted.

"Hello," he called out.

"Good morning," a woman answered . . . but from where? Following the sound of her heavily accented voice to a small curtain-draped cubicle at the back of the store, Javier found a woman who looked even older than his grandmother. Her face was deeply lined and wrinkled, and tufts of kinky gray hair stuck out from under a colorful scarf she'd tied around her head. She was sitting at a table covered in red velvet, carefully laying cards out on the table.

"I am Greta," the woman said without looking up.

Javier introduced himself as the new errand boy and asked her what card game she was playing.

She stopped and stared into his eyes, making Javier feel very uncomfortable. "I am not *playing* anything," Greta answered. "This is a deck of Tarot cards, and one does not play games with it."

Javier moved closer and looked at the cards. They had strange pictures on them. He knew some people believed that Tarot cards could be used to predict the future. "Can you tell my fortune with those things?" he asked.

"I do not need the cards to tell *your* fate," the elderly

woman said mysteriously. "It is here." She held out both hands in the dim light, and Javier stared at her slender, gnarled fingers and age-spotted skin that hung loosely on the backs of her hands. "Your fate was already decided when you walked through that door," she added. "And the only way to avoid it is to leave now before . . . " Suddenly Greta seemed fearful and her gaze shifted to the front door. Javier turned to see Reynaldo standing there.

"Ah, so you are here," he said gruffly to Javier. "Well, you needn't stand idle. Come with me. There are some boxes of books that need to be unpacked."

Javier followed the old man to a cramped, gloomy storeroom filled with cardboard boxes. "Check the contents of these boxes against this list," he said, handing Javier a printed sheet of paper. "When you are finished, you can dust the shelves in the shop." And with that he turned and brushed by the boy, leaving him alone in the dimly lit room.

Javier looked around, then set to work by the light of only one bare light bulb that hung from the ceiling. He opened the first box and peered inside. It was filled with books on sorcery. One small volume in particular caught Javier's attention.

"*The Spells of the Ancients,*" he read aloud, opening the book. As he did, something skittered along the far wall. Alarmed, Javier turned and stared into the shadows, but there was nothing there. "Must be rats," he muttered with a shiver. "I'd better get to work and get out of this gross place." But he really wanted to read a little of the small book he still held in his hands. Then he made a decision. He quickly hid the book under a box so that he could get it later and take it home.

After finishing the chore Reynaldo had given him, Javier

picked up a feather duster that was hanging on a hook on the wall and headed for the main area of the shop to dust the shelves.

As he worked he noticed the people who entered the shop. Some were obviously just curious shoppers. Others seemed a little odd—even creepy. One woman purchased a bag of dried herbs and, muttering something under her breath, took out a pinch, crushed it in her fingers, and sprinkled it over her own hair. Then a man with a patch over one eye asked Javier if the store stocked spider venom! Shuddering, Javier went to ask Reynaldo, noticing that the man kept glancing nervously over his shoulder at the door as if he were afraid of what might enter.

By the afternoon Javier was ready to go home—both because he was tired and because the place had given him a good case of the creeps. Before he left, however, he slipped back to the storeroom once again to retrieve the slim book on sorcery that he had hidden earlier. Making sure that no one could see what he was doing, he tucked the book under his shirt. But when he turned to leave, Javier found himself face to face with Reynaldo.

"I see you are not to be trusted," the aged man growled.

Javier shook his head. "You don't understand," he moaned. "I wasn't stealing it. I was going to bring it back. I just wanted to read it and maybe learn some of the spells."

Reynaldo glared at him. "You might have asked," he said slowly. "But no matter. If you are so desperate to learn a few magical spells, I can grant your desire."

Javier wasn't sure what to say. He thought the man would be angry, and here it seemed Reynaldo was offering to tutor him.

"You look surprised," Reynaldo remarked with a sly grin. "I could show you many things. I assure you, I am a most capable sorcerer." As a demonstration, he pointed one finger at a box on the floor and it slowly rose into the air then began to spin. Javier gasped in stunned amazement. "Yes, I would be willing to share some of my knowledge with you," Reynaldo added. "But of course I would want something . . . in exchange."

Something inside of Javier screamed that he should just put the book down, leave, and never come back. But he couldn't tear his eyes away from the spinning box. He'd give anything to be able to do such things—and here was someone who obviously knew how to teach him.

"What kind of exchange?" Javier asked uneasily, against his better judgment. "You don't mean that you want my soul or something."

Reynaldo tipped back his head and laughed unpleasantly. "No, I would have no use for such a thing," he declared, then looked coldly at Javier. "All I'll take is your time."

"My time?" Javier scowled. It seemed like a strange request in exchange for something so wonderful. *There must be a catch*, he thought to himself, then said, "I'm already working two days, but I guess I could be here after school, too." He grinned at the aged magician. "I'll think about it."

"You do that, my boy," Reynaldo said, grinning back. "And when you decide, just say so wherever you are . . . and I will hear you."

What did he mean by that? Javier thought, leaving the shop for home. As he exited he noticed that Greta was staring at him. She sure was a weird one.

· · · · · · · · · · ·

That night Javier couldn't sleep. On the one hand, more of his time seemed little enough to give for the knowledge that he had always wanted. But on the other hand, Reynaldo kind of scared him. Then he sat up in bed. "What could possibly go wrong?" he said confidently. "I'll do it!"

"Done!" Reynaldo's disembodied voice declared from nowhere and everywhere.

"Huh?" Javier grunted, looking around his bedroom for the source of the voice. And then, to his amazement, he saw a small leather-bound book appear on his night stand. Shaking with fear and excitement, he turned on the light, snatched up the book in his trembling hand, and opened its pages. He read the chapter titles.

"To make flowers bloom from a stick . . . to raise objects . . . to become invisible—this is incredible!" he exclaimed.

All at once the air began to swirl slowly around the room. Trying to control his wildly pounding heart, Javier drew in a terrified breath as the glowing image of Reynaldo appeared. He was dressed as he had been in the old poster.

"You have what you want," the ghostly figure hissed. "But be warned. If you ever show anyone the book or tell them about it, the book and your power will disappear without a trace. And now that our business is done, I will take my leave of you . . . forever."

Abruptly the room was once again quiet and the image of Reynaldo was gone. In awe, Javier stared at the spot where the magician had been, then turned his attention back to the marvelous book. He chose a spell—the spell to raise

objects. He studied it, and pointed his finger at his clock radio. Laughing with delight he watched it rise unsteadily from his dresser. After quickly testing several more spells, Javier finally fell into a blissful sleep, clutching the book of his dreams in his arms.

The sun was just rising when Javier woke again. He couldn't wait to get up and try some of the more exotic enchantments.

My life will never be the same, he thought gleefully as he pushed back the covers. *I won't have to stay here anymore. I can have anything I want.*

He started to get up, then sat awkwardly back on the edge of the bed. He still felt very tired and his fingers were a little stiff. *They probably hurt from holding the book,* he reasoned, rubbing his knuckles. But when he looked down at his hands, a shock coursed through his entire body. His fingers were slender and gnarled, and the loose skin on the backs of his hands was spotted with age.

All at once, the image of Greta, the old fortune-teller in the shop, came back clearly. He could see her holding out her hands to him. "Your fate is here," she had said—and now he knew why she had made a point of showing him her time-worn hands.

"No! It can't be true!" Javier pleaded. In terror he raced to the mirror and stared in disbelief at the image of a wrinkled old man. "My time!" he cried out. "Reynaldo took *all* of my time!"